MINISTERS AND PRISONERS

JEREMY AAL

WARNING:
this book contains adult language

Book statistics
Page size.................6"x9"
Pages.....................127
Words....................42,474

MINISTERS AND PRISONERS
Published by: Jeremy Aal.
Copyright © 2020 by Jeremy Aal.
All rights reserved.

ISBN: 978-1-7 338 952-6-2

www.ministersbook.com

The voice of one crying in the wilderness
Isaiah 40:3 NKJV

Sirs, I perceive that this voyage will be with hurt
and much damage,
not only of the lading and ship,
but also of our lives.

Acts 27:10 KJV

1

Erik was closing the door behind him when he saw his mother sitting in her over-sized recliner. She sat stoically at the corner of the small living room, a half-dozen cigarette butts stamped out on the end table beside her. The teenage boy locked eyes with the expressionless woman, unable to decide if she already knew. *Play it safe*, he thought to himself.

"Hi, Mom. No work today?" He asked with a fake curious tone.

"Strange. You know, I really wanted to work today but I couldn't. I got a call from your school, again. Seems like you didn't work today, either," she said sarcastically. Her face remained still.

Damn. "What do you mean?" He asked again in a curious tone even less believable than before.

The woman's neutral face began to sour. "You know exactly what I mean, Erik Francis." Her voice became increasingly tainted with anger as her eyes began to squint and her lips puckered. "There I was, spending my whole morning getting ready for my shift when what do I get? A phone call from the school letting me know that you weren't in class today and that you were suspended for skipping!"

Well, guess I'm screwed either way. Erik took a deep breath, put on a smile, and met her with sarcasm. "Seems kind of backwards to me – giving a kid a day off of school as punishment for not showing up."

The woman's face turned more foul. "You think this is funny? How do you think I feel? My son is a truant and the whole school knows it. First you start skipping school, then what? Huh? What next? Are you going to start stealing cars and robbing banks?" The angry words came out faster and with fury. "I just can't believe you, Erik. You were such a good boy and now you are fixing yourself up to be common criminal. What are the girls at the diner going to think? Huh? Did you even think of that? 'Hey girls, here comes Bethany, the mom who raised a convict.' What do you think about that?" She was now scooted to the edge of her stained recliner, eyes piercing the boy's face.

Erik stepped back from the words and hit the door knob with his hip. "Mom, chill out. I just didn't want to go to school today..." the boy said in defense before being cut-off.

"I don't care what your excuses are. They're probably all lies, anyway. What do you have to say for yourself? Making me the laughing stock at work? Do you not like food? What do you think will happen if I keep missing work? We can just not feed you for a while and see if you still feel like making me call off?"

The woman stood up from the chair and stomped swiftly toward her son still standing with his back against the door. Stopping a foot away, her arms on her hips, the woman looked down at him. He was fifteen years old but she was still taller than him – even if only by an inch.

He said nothing and looked at the corner of the ceiling.

"Look at me when I am talking to you!"

He said nothing and tilted his head as if he had a new thought.

The woman reached for the boy's jaw with her bony hand, grabbed it tightly and jerked his head inline with hers. "Look at me when I am talking to you," she said quietly but with a sternness that gave the boy goosebumps. Erik looked down at the dry and cracked hand grasping his jaw. He could smell the nicotine on her skin.

"Well?" She asked with fake sincerity.

Erik looked up and into the woman's eyes. They were tired and bloodshot and the whites were slightly yellowed, an apologetic companion to her decade of heavy smoking. Her green eyes were once as holy and mysterious as the coastal forest the family used to explore. Erik once looked into his mother's eyes and saw lush moss growing thick on nurse logs and fields of grass and wildflowers. Now he sees nothing in them but bitterness and disdain, spite for every person in her life. Every living person and every living thing and everything she saw was a malevolent threat to her existence. Erik continued to look into the woman's eyes. He looked for answers but found none.

"I'm waiting," she said raising her eyebrows forcing a lop-sided smile.

Erik continued his stare at her – through her. His face would have bled pain if his jaw was not held tight in the woman's hand. The woman grew impatient with the boy and her face returned to its previous scorn. She squeezed the boy's jaw and shook it. An audible thunk came from the door as his skull hit the wood. Erik reflexively pushed the woman's hand off of his face and away from him, pushing the woman back with his other hand in the same reflexive motion. The woman was startled by the boy's reaction.

She lost her balance and fell backwards tripping over her shoes near the door. She fell onto the ground where she laid for a moment confused at what had just occurred. Shocked, Erik looked down at the woman laying on the floor, unsure of what just happened or what he should do, unsure of what she would do. She then looked up at him and a wicked snarl set into her face. She took a deep breath preparing to unleash her rage at the boy for hitting her and pushing her to the ground. Erik saw this and grabbed at the door knob and turned it, swinging the door open. He spun and ran out the door, jumping the three steps off the sagging plywood porch and continued running down the circular drive of the trailer park. The woman followed him out the door and cursed him from the porch. "You bastard! Yeah, you run away you little bitch! You're a little bitch and you know it! Just like your father! You just wait until Ed hears what you did to me and..." Her hysterical voice shrank as Erik ran down the dirt court and onto the paved road and down the road away from the row of mobile homes.

Erik continued at a full run for a mile down the road until he came to the community park which separated the sprawling suburban development from the untamed wilds of the Chugach mountains butting against the civil expanse. He ran on the well-maintained gravel trail that meandered its way through the seldom used park. He ran off the maintained trail and down through the willow-brush which grew thick alongside. Stumbling over roots and uneven ground, Erik ran through the dense shrubs until he came to a ravine with a trickle of water at the bottom of it. Wheezing and with shaking legs and hands, Erik worked his way down to the water and made a cup with his hands and sipped from them and wet his lips and wet his face. He coughed up some water and fought to catch his breath. Looking up the ravine he saw a familiar shelf formed by the soil eroding from the bank of the creek. It was at a turn in the creek but just higher than the water and was dry inside. He approached the small, boy-sized hole-in-the-wall of the bank and crawled in, curling his knees into his chest so he could sit up with his back against the crumbling wall. Erik took a deep breath and looked westward down the ravine cut by the small, slow-moving trickle of water – just as he had done most of that day.

2

Erik sat against the dirt wall watching the cloudy sky turn pink and purple with the setting sun. His legs were cold and numb from lack of blood flow. His knees were bent sharply at their joints and curled into his chest. His fingers and toes began to burn in the early December chill. There was no snow on the ground and the days were pleasant if the sun was out. If the sun hid behind cloudy skies, the chill was hard to shake. The deep sky became lively as the oranges and reds and purples teased of the concealed sun. The boy watched the clouds and he watched the sky. He watched chickadees and grosbeaks and wintering birds of all kinds fly across the sky and dive into trees, back into the sky, then into a neighboring tree. He watched a squirrel run from one side of the ravine to the other, looking for any last seeds to add to its cache. He listened as a doe and her fawn moved through the brush higher in the ravine, out of his sight. The deer stepped carefully, listening for predators as they moved from where they bedded earlier that day. They moved to find vegetation, any vegetation that was not brown and dead in the transitioning season. They continued their search, a desperate search, but winter was still to come. Erik sat and he watched and he listened, and he thought.

Why? Why me? Why her? Who is this woman? What happened to us? We were all so happy and so fun and now, now it's all shit. Everything. My mom is shit. My dad is shit. My whole family is shit. Should I call the cops? Maybe Mom will come and apologize? I remember her so warm and now she is so cold. She changed into this monster but she could change back. She just doesn't understand what she is doing! Who am I kidding? Listen to yourself, Erik. She isn't going to change. She knows what she is doing. She ran Dad off and now she's run me off. I don't know... I don't know what to think. Who am I supposed to ask for help? Dad? He is an adult and married the witch and still couldn't handle her. How's he expect me to handle her? Last time I called him he just said 'stop making her mad'. Jesus Christ. Easy for him to say. He's only in town twice a year. Erik released his hands from hugging his thighs, raised his palms up, shrugged his shoulder and mocked, "she is just trying the best she can. Give me a break." The sarcasm left his nostrils flared and his upper lip curled to one side. He laughed once out of indignation.

The boy sat in silence and wandered in his mental chambers until the sun set over the distant mountains behind the clouds. He began to shiver under his sweater. The loosely-woven fabric was insufficient against the cold earth he was pressed against. He was proud of the red and white reindeer pattern pull-over and found comfort wearing the scratchy wool gift even when the Alaskan winter demanded much heavier layers.

Erik closed his eyes, took in a deep breath, held it, and slowly released the air through pursed lips. With careful movement he angled one leg out from the tight, make-shift den and extended the leg against stiff muscles. He turned his body slightly and angled the other leg and extended it. With a low groan, Erik shifted his whole body and half-rolled out from under the shelf, got to his knees and stood up. His knees and back ached from hours in a cramped position. Rotating his head from side to side, several loud cracks came from his neck releasing tension. Curling his toes inside his shoes, Erik struggled to get sensation back to his numb feet. After another moment of silence, he began walking in the direction from which he came. First stepping across the small creek and working up the loose embankment which framed the ravine, Erik then stepped more carefully through the dense willows until he found the well-maintained gravel trail. He began walking the trail toward the entrance of the park where he would follow the road back to his house.

~

Few cars drove passed the boy as he walked along the residential side-street. Now dark as the early-winter sun was far below the horizon, only drug-dealers and drunkards drove on the cracked pavement. A set of headlights came from behind Erik and slowed to his pace. The dark vehicle approached the boy and the driver rolled down the window.

"Erik Larsen?" The driver asked clearly from inside the crawling vehicle.

Erik turned and looked at the dark figure inside the car. The driver was silhouetted against several small screens fixed to the dash and center console.

"I am Officer Browne with the Anchorage Police Department. Are you Erik?" The man asked tactfully but with noticeable concern.

"What do you want?" Erik asked.

"Your mother called and said you ran away. She is worried about you.

We've been looking for you all evening."

"What else did she say?"

"I don't know, kid. She is probably worried about you and wants to know you are safe. Come with me and I'll take you home."

"Yeah. I bet she is real worried." Erik didn't look at the man and kept walking on the edge of the road.

"Come on, Erik. Your mom is worried sick. I need to take you back home so you two can work out whatever problems you got," the officer pleaded.

Erik's pace remained constant.

"Erik. I have to take you back home. Please stop and get in the car and I will drive you back home."

Erik's pace remained constant.

"Alright, man. We tried this the easy way." Officer Browne stopped the car, put it in Park, opened the driver's door and stepped out. The officer towered over the boy and had a stout build. Officer Browne took a few quick steps toward Erik and grabbed his arm. Erik tugged at the man and freed his arm from the loose grip and kept walking his previous pace. Officer Browne grabbed Erik's arm again but with a much tighter grip. Erik jolted to a stop and tried to jerk his arm again but the officer's grip won the short-lived battle. "Come on, Erik. Come with me."

Officer Browne was obviously irritated with the boy's lack of compliance. He began to pull the squirming boy as Erik resisted walking in the direction of the patrol car. Officer Browne kept walking toward the car and tugged the boy by the arm until the man's temper started to break. The officer stopped, pulled the boy around to his front and the man stood straight with his head tilted down over the boy. He grabbed the boy's other arm with his free hand and held both of Erik's arms with a tight grip and shook him twice and raised his voice. "Stop it, kid! I was nice with you at first but I am going to stop being nice to you if you don't knock it off. Now what's it going to be?"

"Fine! I was walking back home, anyway," Erik said with disgust.

The pair turned toward the car and the officer loosened his grip on the boy's arm. As the two walked the last few steps to the patrol car, Officer Browne released his grip from Erik, opened the door behind the driver's, and put his hand on Erik's head as he sat on the backseat and brought his legs forward. The officer made sure the boy's hands and feet were inside the rear compartment and closed the door. He then opened the driver's door, sat in the front seat, and grabbed the radio microphone announcing "the missing subject has been found."

A mile separated the patrol car and the trailer park. The drive was a brief encounter. The officer said nothing to the boy and the boy said nothing to the officer. There was nothing to say. The boy was soured that his mother called the police, a tool she was becoming fond of. The officer was soured that his shift had been spent looking for a runaway kid in the ghettos of the urban hub where an officer was more likely to be spat on or have a rock thrown at his car rather than on the highway where his ticket quota would be met.

Officer Browne looked in the rear-view mirror at Erik and said, "you shouldn't be running off and worrying your mother. You know how many resources are being spent on you? Everyone in the city doesn't need to pay for your mistakes. I don't know what problems you got with your mother but you need to get your act together." Officer Browne paused, then continued, "I recommend you tell your mother you're sorry and see if you can't patch things up while you're still young. If you keep worrying her like this you're going to have hell to pay." The man flashed his eyes in the mirror again, "What's this all about, kid?"

Erik said in a hushed, emotionless voice, "that woman is a witch." Almost as if a matter-of-fact.

Officer Browne brought his eyes back to the road. Under his breath he uttered, "I'm sure she is a real piece of work." The two were quiet for the remainder of the short drive.

As the patrol car circled in the driveway, Erik's mother came out of the house. In a slight panic, she quickly stepped down from the porch and toward the vehicle. Officer Browne stepped out as the woman approached.

She said, "oh, thank you officer. I was just beside myself."

"Don't thank me, ma'am. Erik is safe and sound." Officer Browne stepped to the rear door and opened it.

The woman reached for Erik's arm before he could step out of the vehicle. The slight tug was a surprise and he lost his balance. "Oh honey, I missed you! Where did you go? I can't believe you would just run off like that. You scared me half to death," she said with heavy concern. The sweetness stung Erik's ears.

"Thank you, officer. I am sure this won't happen again. Now say 'thank you' to the officer for bringing you home, Erik," she said as Officer Browne closed the rear door and sat back inside the patrol car. Erik walked back to the house without addressing him.

As he drove away, Officer Browne looked once more in the rear-view mirror at the mother and son standing on the porch. He said to himself, "yeah, a real snake." He scoffed once, brought his eyes back to the road, and drove away.

The woman followed Erik inside the house and closed the door behind them. Erik kicked off his shoes by the door and began to walk toward his room.

"Hey! Where d'ya think you're goin'?" A large man in his 40's sat in an upright chair across the room. He glared at Erik and called at him again as the boy started to walk. Erik stopped and looked over to the man. *Great...*

"I heard ya like to beat up women," the man said. He set the cheap beer he was holding on the end table, knocking two empty cans onto the floor joining several others. The man struggled up from the chair balancing his protruding gut, then approached Erik who stood motionless looking toward the corner of the ceiling.

The man stopped a foot from the boy, lifted his hand and pointed a thick finger in Erik's face. "You ungrateful piece'a shit. Yer mother works 'er ass off keepin' this place in order and ya thank 'er by knocking 'er lights out? Well, how 'bout ya pick on someone yer own size?" Erik looked up at the spitting man. His breath was nauseating.

After a moment of silence, the man pushed Erik sideways against the wall. Erik put his arms up pushing the man's hand away. The man scowled and with one grunt he used his forearm to push the boy hard against the wall and held him there.

The woman ran over to the man and put her hands on his shoulder and chest, "Ed! It's okay dear. It wasn't that big of a deal, anyway."

Ed looked at the woman and elbowed her back with his free arm. He said slowly at the woman, "did he hit you or not, Beth?" Spittle rained on her as he enunciated.

Bethany pleaded, "well, yes, but I am sure it was just an accident."

"Maybe now's a good time for an education. Maybe he might learn a little respect, huh?"

Erik looked straight at the man and into his dark eyes. Erik struggled for half a breath, then said with emphasis, "respect is earned."

Ed smiled at the boy. "Ya know, kid, I think we finally have somethin' we can agree on." He let his arm down and took a half-step back. Erik coughed and bent at the hip trying to inhale deeply. He looked back at the man. Ed turned slightly, tilting his head and raising both eyebrows suggesting the boy may pass. Erik continued looking intently into the man's eyes and cautiously took one step. With no motion from the man, Erik lifted his foot to take another cautious step. His eyes jumped back to Ed as the man's fist made contact with Erik's jaw. The boy fell sideways onto the floor but he failed to catch himself with his hands. Bethany took two steps closer to the man, her arms straight down, fists clenched, shoulders raised, and cried, "stop it! Stop it right now you two!"

Erik pushed his chest off the floor by his elbows, turned his head and looked up at the man with disgust. The man looked down at the boy and smiled. Erik wiped one hand along his lower lip now wet with blood. Erik stood up, looked once more at the man who now appeared to be laughing under his breath, then turned and walked toward the hallway leading to his bedroom. As Erik opened the door, Ed yelled down the hall, "now you're gunna come back here and clean up this mess you left 'fore I get back or we're gunna have another lesson!"

Once the bedroom door closed behind Erik, Ed walked to the front door and put on his jacket. He stepped out the door and shut it in the woman's face as she tried to follow him. She opened the door, stepped out, and watched him as he walked toward his old truck sitting along side the house. Bethany called from the porch, "what did you do that for?"

Ed put one foot in the truck, held himself stable with the steering wheel, and said without looking at the woman, "earnin' a little respect in this house."

Bethany called again from the porch, "the school's going to be asking about that split lip!"

The man, still holding himself half in the truck, looked at the woman and said, "that's your problem." He grunted as he pulled himself the rest of the way in the truck and started the old motor. He backed the vehicle out of the driveway, put it in Drive and sped away.

Listening to the truck rumble through the thin walls, Erik stood in the bathroom and studied himself in the mirror. He looked into his own blue eyes and then at his lip. He watched the blood run from the inside of his mouth, down to his chin and drip to the sink. Each red drop stained the porcelain and a halo of lava radiated to the drain. Without moving his eyes off his wounded reflection, Erik pulled his phone from his jeans pocket, swiped his thumb across the screen to open the camera and brought it up to his side. Tapping the screen, he heard the shutter noise twice and looked at the images. Satisfied with their content, he returned the device to his pocket. For several more moments he studied his reflection in the mirror. He noticed how his light brown hair had darkened since its summertime blonde. He noticed his unchanging, clear complexion. He noticed his angular jaw. He then noticed his damaged lip beginning to swell. Erik washed his face, then walked quietly back to his room where he sat on his bed in silence before falling asleep.

Surely I am more stupid than any man,
And do not have the understanding of a man.
Proverbs 30:2 NKJV

3

Erik sat at the head of his bed with his back against the wall. His head hung down and he looked at a blank sheet of paper on his lap. He played with the pencil he held in his left hand, rolling it between his thumb and middle finger. For several moments he looked at the blank page in front of him before turning his head toward the morning light.

Looking out the window of his small room, he could see a magpie sitting on the fence separating their mobile home from the next. He observed the scavenging bird, its cautious watch over the neighborhood looking for scraps of food dragged out of garbage bags by a half-feral dog. He observed its order of movement as is hopped from one plank of wood to the next. He observed its black face and wings and its white breast. He observed a single green-iridescent feather blending into its black tail. *What an interesting creature.*

His focus was broken when he heard his doorknob rattle. His mother opened the door quickly as if she hoped to catch him in the middle of a wrongful act. She stepped in the room with an expression between kindness and concern. Stopping in front of the bed, she looked at Erik and asked sweetly, "how are you feeling, honey?"

Erik looked away from the woman and back to the fence but the bird was gone. "Fine," he said looking at the now vacant fence top.

"You know, it is getting really close to Christmas break. Just a few more days," she said.

Erik continued his gaze into the distance.

"Are you all packed and ready to go to your father's?"

"I guess," Erik said dismissively.

"Well, I was thinking... I know you have been under a lot of stress lately and, you know, we all need to take a vacation every now and then to recharge the batteries. How would you feel about maybe going to Kodiak a little early?" She paused, studying his absent reaction. "You only have three days of school left anyway and I'm sure your teachers would understand. I can write them a note and explain you left a few days sooner than planned for a family vacation." *Family vacation.*

He turned his head back to the woman. Her eyes moved between his eyes and his swollen lip, and back to his eyes. His left jaw began to show a faint bruising under his pale skin. He broke the silence, "why are you doing this?"

"Honey, I just thought maybe you would want to spend some extra time with your father. I know you enjoy holidays with him so much and all of those deserts he makes you and those Norwegian Christmas songs you sing together."

"Is this what you want, Mom?"

"Erik, honey, I love you. I just want what's best for you."

Erik looked down at the blank paper on his lap, thought for a moment, then looked back at her. He ran his tongue over the spot where his lip split and he felt the healing scab. "When can I leave?" He asked.

"You can leave today if you like. I'll go get your tickets moved." The woman turned and walked toward the door. Erik watched her leave and saw a stride of satisfaction.

The woman walked carefully down the hall and into her room. She closed the door behind her and stepped to the orderly desk beside her bed. She picked up two sheets of paper from the top of a small stack next to the printer. She held the amended confirmation against her chest and sighed in relief. She walked back to the kitchen and placed the papers on the counter and proceeded to make a warm breakfast.

~

"Now are you sure you have everything? You have your toothbrush and toothpaste and extra socks and underwear?" Bethany asked as she drove through the short-term lot near the airport terminal.

Erik sighed heavily and replied, "yeah, Mom. I told you before we left. I have everything."

"Well, maybe I should check just in case. You are always forgetting something."

"Mom, I have everything I need. If I forgot something, which I didn't, I have spares at Dad's, anyway."

Bethany pulled into a vacant spot, put the transmission in Park, and turned the key. She looked at Erik and shook one finger in his face and said, "what if he used something while you were gone and didn't replace it? That's just the kind of thing he might do. I really ought to check and make sure you have everything in your bag."

"If Dad used up all of the soap, then I will walk to the store and buy soap. I have everything I need. Please stop worrying. I will be fine. Can we please just go?" Erik asked with unhidden frustration.

Bethany looked at Erik, then looked at the darkening bruise along his jaw. "Well, then come along and get your things. You don't want to be late and miss your flight."

As the two approached the terminal, Erik slowed and gazed at the massive structure. His eyes followed the curved roof line of the building to its edge, then followed the white, metal awning back. The wall of windows in front of him glowed and helped light the covered sidewalk. The mid-December sun hung low in the sky and little light came through the clouds leaving the arctic hub dull. The sky was grey. The building was grey. The cement was grey. Everything looked void of life.

A sudden noise startled Erik and his eyes instinctively searched for the source.

"Come on, Erik. What are you standing there for?" Bethany repeated from the covered sidewalk. Erik quickly looked down and realized he had stopped in the middle of the crosswalk and two cars were now waiting for him to move. "I say, Erik. You are a strange boy. What has gotten into you?" She rhetorically asked under her breath.

They walked down the line of ticket counters toward the hallway marked **ALL GATES**. As they approached the security line, Bethany turned and looked at Erik inspecting him from top to bottom. "Okay. You have your pass. You have your bag. Are you sure you aren't forgetting anything?" She asked as her hands reached for the pack on Erik's back.

Erik turned from her reach and said, "yes, I have everything I need. I have done this a hundred times, I know what to do."

"Erik, you are fifteen years old. You are the child and I am the parent. I want what is best for you. Do you know where to go? I want to make sure you don't get lost, again. This summer was the first time you flew by yourself and do I need to remind you what happened? You weren't through security ten minutes before they found you wandering half-way across the terminal!"

"Jesus, Mom. For the last time, I wasn't lost. I was just walking around killing time," Erik said annoyed. "Then that blue-haired whale started yelling at me and wouldn't let me walk back by myself."

"That is no way to talk about a security officer. If it wasn't for that nice lady you might still be lost hiding in a broom closet!"

Erik said under his breath, almost inaudibly, "the only thing cow-face kept secure was the food court."

Bethany stood with her hands on her hips and inspected the boy once more. She licked two fingers and started to tame a wild hair from Erik's cowlick but he turned his head and pulled away from her. "Alright. Give mommy a hug and a kiss." She reached forward and embraced Erik. He turned his head to the right and kept his arms to his side. As the woman leaned to give her son a kiss on the cheek she stopped. Noticing the bruise along his jaw line, she awkwardly stretched her neck and gave a quick peck high on Erik's cheek near his ear then let go. "I already talked with your father and he is going to be at the baggage claim waiting for you. If anything happens you call me. And call me as soon as you land. Okay? I love you, honey. Enjoy your Christmas break!"

Erik said nothing. He started toward the line flowing to security but was held back by his hand. Bethany continued to hold onto Erik's hand by the wrist and tugged it once more looking directly at his eyes.

Erik asked, "what do you want?"

"Didn't you forget something? I told you 'I love you' but you didn't say anything back. Now tell me you love me," she demanded sweetly.

Erik took a deep breath and said, "I love you, Mom. I will let you know when the plane lands."

"Okay. Now you run along. I will wait here until you are all the way through security."

She let go of his wrist and Erik turned once again to the line. He stood in line and crept forward with the crowd. Once to the officer who sat at the origin of the line, Erik handed him his ID and printed boarding pass. The officer inspected it, handed it back, and waived him along with a hushed grunt.

Erik drifted his way toward the gate. He walked slowly and looked out the wall of glass at the distant Chugach mountains to the east. The dusk light colored the range and each mountain become well-defined. As he moved along the wall of glass, the wall of grey and purple rock moved, too. The terrain became textured as the sun lowered in the western sky. The buildings became taller against the mountains and the mountains became taller against the horizon. As the horizon consumed the sun, the mountains fell from the horizon and the buildings fell from the mountains. Erik watched the final moments of life escape the mountains and he watched them became faint and hazy. He silently mourned the dying wall of rock and as the light disappeared from the sky, blackness appeared in the wall of glass. Erik continued looking into the wall of glass but he now saw only a reflection of himself standing with his back to the crowd.

Arriving at the gate, Erik found an empty row of chairs and sat down. He placed his backpack between his legs and pulled his phone out from his jeans pocket. He opened a new message:

Mom: remember to call when u land! Luv u!!!

He tapped back and opened another message:

Dad: Hey buddy. Your mom says you are coming today instead of Saturday like planned. I told her I would pick you up but I won't be back to Kodiak until tomorrow. Don't tell your mom! You know where the key is. Should be food in the freezer.

Erik shook his head and scoffed. "The war never ends…" he said lightly. He put the phone back in his pocket, folded his hands on his lap, closed his eyes and waited for the lady to call for boarding. Erik rested his body and observed his fellow travelers.

~

Hello, Stranger. We have not met before. I do not know you. Before now, I never could have conceived of you. I could not see your face. I could not hear your voice. I could not feel your touch. I could not share your laughter. I could not learn from your wisdom. I could not conceive of you. Now that I know you, I cannot conceive of not knowing you. I have seen your face. I have heard your voice. I have felt your touch. I have shared your laughter. I have learned from your wisdom. You have changed me. You have altered something fundamental within me. I am not the same man anymore. Nothing about me is the same. When I did not know you, you were nothing to me. Before we met, you did not exist. You breathed, you laughed, you spoke, you lived, but I knew none of it. When our meeting adjourns and we part ways, wherever you are in the world, I know you. You are a blessed creation and I have never met anyone like you. You have a family. You are somebody's child. You have a mother who taught you. You have a father who trained you. You have a mother who worries and you have a father who is vulnerable. You have lived a powerful life, one with meaning and purpose. You pursued great things. You have surmounted great obstacles. You are full of mystery and wonder. Our time together is small. I have only a short while to appreciate your challenges and relish your victories. Our time together is limited but your impact is eternal. I shall forever know you, Stranger. Your words will whisper in the wind, your touch will tremble in the earth, your spirit will warm in the sun. You have left a scar on my heart. Wherever my path may lead, you shall accompany me.

~

Erik sat two rows from the rear of the plane. He was one of the first people in line to board, found his seat, and watched the remaining travelers find their seats.

A middle-aged man wearing a black suit fought with his rolling travel bag in Business Class. The hard edges caught on the seats as he walked down the aisle until he picked the bag up and shoved it into the overhead storage. Five rows behind the business man, a young couple soothed their newborn child. The baby fussed and wailed. The young mother hummed to the baby and the young father rested his hand on the back of the baby's head caressing its sparse white hair. Three rows behind the young couple, two men wore camouflage jackets and well-worn bluejeans. The men joked and laughed. Seven rows behind the friendly gentlemen, a woman and her teenage daughter sat quietly next to each other, faces lit by the soft glow of phones. Erik watched the passengers as they boarded the plane. He watched and he wondered. *Where did you come from? Where will you go?*

"Excuse me young man. I have the window seat," an old, grey woman said to Erik. He looked up at her with some surprise, looked at the two empty seats to this right, then looked back.

"Oh, sure. Here, let me stand up," he said.

"Alright." The old woman stepped back to give Erik room to stand. She shuffled her feet carefully sideways and worked herself to the window seat. As she sat and began fussing with her seat belt, she said without making eye contact, "I appreciate it dear. I always find the most awkward part of flying is having someone wave their fanny in my face." The old woman finally worked the buckle together, looked to Erik and extended her hand. "I am Rosemary. Rosemary Howard."

Erik met the woman's hand and said, "Erik. Nice to meet you, Ms. Howard."

"Oh my dear Erik. Please call me Rosemary," she replied with a chuckle. "Where is your destination?"

"Kodiak. My dad lives there. Are you stopping in Kodiak, too?" Erik asked.

"No, dear. I am changing planes, then going to Unalaska tonight," Rosemary replied.

"That's a long trip. Why are you going all the way to Unalaska?" Erik asked.

"My son and his wife live there. I am staying with them over the holidays," she replied.

Erik looked down at the floor and flexed his toes a few times inside his shoes, then rested his feet flat on the carpet. "How long has it been since you last saw them?"

"It was this last summer when they had their fourth child. I stayed with them for all of June and most of July. James, my son, he works for one of the fishing outfits there in Dutch Harbor. He works so much in the summer busy season so I helped Sarah with the little ones and they seem to enjoy having me around," she replied.

Erik cocked his head in curiosity and smiled. "Four kids? That is kind of a lot these days."

"Yes, it is. And it is so sad to see. Raising children is such a rewarding challenge." Rosemary looked forward, then up to the corner of an imaginary room as if recalling a series of pleasant memories. She chuckled once before her smile drifted away. "Do you have any siblings, Erik?" She asked.

"No. Just me," he replied.

"Do you have any cousins or family your own age?"

"I have a few but they don't live around here." Erik looked up as a stewardess walked by closing the overhead bins brushing his shoulder with her hip. He turned in his seat to face Rosemary, again.

"Oh. Where do they live? Do you call them often?"

Erik broke eye contact and looked out the window behind her. The baggage cart was pulling away and out of his view. He looked back to the old woman and her concerned gaze. He took a deep breath and let it out slowly. "Not really. I have two cousins in Europe. I email with one sometimes but we aren't super close. I also have a cousin in California but I have never met her."

"I see. Is that where part of your family is from? Europe?" Rosemary asked cheerfully.

"Yeah. My dad is from Norway. He was born there then moved to Seattle when he was twenty. He was hired on a fishing crew there and then moved to Alaska when he was offered a better job. His two sisters stayed in Norway to look after my grandparents and their farm," Erik replied.

"That sounds like quite the adventure. What caused him to move all the way across the world? They fish in Norway, don't they?" She asked with genuine interest.

Erik thought for a moment. "I don't exactly know. His parents wanted him to run the farm but he wasn't interested. He moved to the coast and found work on a ship after he graduated from school. He liked it a lot more than farming and told his parents he wasn't come back. I guess they told him that he should just never come back, so he packed his bag and left. At least, that's what I've pieced together anyway. He doesn't talk about that kind of stuff very much." He looked back down to his hands and laced his fingers in his lap.

"What a tragedy," she said softly shaking her head. "Do you know why his parents didn't support his decision to do something else?"

"Nope. Well, they are really traditional people so they probably wanted him as their only son to take over the family farm. They were really supportive later, though."

The old woman looked at him with a neutral face. "What do you think changed?" She asked.

"I don't know. They got back in contact about the time I was born," he replied.

"Interesting. What do you think about that?"

"I think it is pretty dumb to blow up a relationship for that reason alone. After that, the family was never the same," Erik replied.

"Are you sure that was the only reason for their conflict?" She asked.

"I guess I don't know for sure." Erik looked forward again. The stewardess was preparing to start the safety lecture.

"Well, Erik, do you think their relationship was good before your dad moved away?"

"Probably not," he replied deadpan.

"Do you talk with your grandparents much?" Rosemary asked.

"I did. I used to write to my grandfather once a month for as long as I can remember, but he died last spring." Erik glanced at the stewardess demonstrating the belt buckle. He ignored her and listened again to Rosemary.

"I am so sorry to hear that, dear. What did you talk about with him?"

Erik smiled, "all kinds of things. What it was like growing up, the differences between living here and there. Sometimes I'd ask him advice on a problem that I didn't want to talk with my parents about. But mostly I liked hearing about what life was like on their farm."

"Now that is something truly special," Rosemary said. She smiled, exaggerating deep wrinkles in her face. "I'll give you a little secret: old people love talking with young people. Most young people just aren't interested in talking with us. Good conversations is a dying art, I'm afraid to say." Her smile faded into a deep, complicated expression.

"I don't fit in well with most guys my age. So many kids my age are just fixed to their screens. I feel like I can't connect with any of them. That's why I enjoy talking with older people so much. I hardly feel like I can connect with anyone else."

"Just please be careful not to put an entire age-group up on a pedestal. After all, we are largely at fault for not transferring those values to your generation," she warned.

"I guess, but still..."

The stewardess completed her lecture while the plane taxied. They both looked forward and sat straight in their seats.

"Oh, I just love this part," Rosemary said gleefully.

The pilot turned the plane and followed the unseen lines of paint and pavement. The whine from the jets increased. A low thunder rumbled, then came a violent thrust pushing the passengers into their seats. The scene outside the windows moved increasingly quick. An imaginary force pulled the people downward as the plane rose into the sky. After only a few seconds, the show was over. Erik looked back to Rosemary who had an inaudible excitement across her face. Her thrill was short-lived. The smile faded again and she let out a little chuckle, "I'll never tire of that feeling." She took a deep breath and looked back to Erik and turned in her seat to face him. "Now, you said your father lives in Kodiak. Does you mother live in Anchorage?" She asked.

"Yeah. I live with her most of the time. Only on holidays do I stay with my dad, like Christmas break and sometimes in the summer for a week."

"Are they divorced? Is that right?"

"Yup. When I was five. Dad moved out to Kodiak and that was that," he replied.

"I am really sorry to hear that, Erik. That's such a pity."

"Hey, it wasn't your fault. You have nothing to be sorry for," he said.

"I can empathize without taking blame. I am sorry you went through such an experience."

"It got better afterward, so at least it brought some peace." Erik shrugged and looked out the window and watched the arctic metropolis shrink between the mountains and the sea.

"Then I am sorry you had so much turmoil before the divorce, though I would bet it was probably still hard after, just in a different way. You need the right kind of peace."

"I guess you're right," he said.

"How is your relationship with your father, if you don't mind me asking?"

"I don't mind. I think it is okay. We could be closer but it isn't bad," he replied.

"Do you mean physically closer or emotionally closer?"

Erik sighed. "Both. I wish I could know him a little more."

"What do you mean?" She asked.

"I don't know. I guess, I guess I just don't know him. How difficult would it be to connect with someone who has been absent from your life? Especially from the age of five? That's when fathers start to become so much more important in a child's life! I feel like a boy who was raised by women."

"Right..." she said. "Right."

~

The aging 737 shook with turbulence. Long, black streaks of corrosion and filth ran back from the rivets and the seams cutting along the aluminum wings. The fuselage was sad and moaned as it rose and fell in the tumultuous columns of air. The aircraft moved south, then southwest. To the east, the Kenai mountains stood sharp against the sea. Rugged peaks were white with snow which trailed along the ridges and shoulders and abruptly ended at the deep fjords outlining the mountainous peninsula. Glaciers flowing from the fjords cracked and bottomless crevasses worked through the fields of ice like an endless, haunted road. Once green and teeming with life, the hillsides now stood grey and frozen. To the west, a long chain of volcanoes stood out of the sea. Brown walls of rock separated fields of ash. At the base of the volcanoes ran a maze of rivers and lakes reclaiming the desolate territory. Land which was once green and healthy and supported great life was assaulted with molten rock and acidic ash. As the years became decades became centuries, the moonscape underwent a metamorphosis and awoke to find new life, life returning to it, rebuilding it. Mountains and glaciers became volcanic domes and craters. Brown hills eroded into dull valleys. The valleys grew into brown hills and those hills became walls of rock and those walls became glaciers and those glaciers became green mountains facing the sea and along the sea the Aleutian islands rose. Cased between the mountains and fjords of the east and the volcanoes and islands of the west, the aging vessel droned over Cook Inlet and toward to sea. The water was dark reflecting the opaque winter sky.

The plane approached the rocky island of Kodiak and small dots of light twinkled along the shoreline marking its edge from an abyss.

~

"Why dear Erik, it seems we have talked ourselves all the way to Kodiak. Thank you so much for the delightful conversation and sharing so much with me. It is an honor and a privilege to know you," Rosemary said with joy.

"I am really glad I met you, Rosemary. I wish we had more time together," Erik said.

"Me, too. But nothing great lasts forever on this earth. We all have our own lives to live. That is why it is so important to cherish the moments we have together and learn from each other when we have the opportunity. There isn't enough time in this life for small talk. Maybe the next life will be different."

The plane taxied up the runway and came to a stop near a small building with off-white metal sides. Erik pulled his backpack up from between his knees and into his lap, waiting for his turn to stand. Once the cabin was nearly clear, he stood and slid on his pack. He extended a hand to Rosemary who was lifting herself to her feet. She grabbed his hand and said, "oh, thank you dear. After sitting for so long my legs are a little cramped," as she side-stepped from under the overhead bins. Erik reached for her single bag in the compartment and set it down next to her.

"May I carry your bag?" He asked.

"Oh, no. I do need some kind of exercise," she said with a pleasant chuckle. "You are such a gentleman. Why aren't more young men like you?"

Erik walked slowly toward the exit of the plane where the stewardess smiled. "You have a wonderful day, Mr. Larsen," she said with an adoring smile.

"Thank you, ma'am. You have a wonderful day, too," he replied, then looked back down the plane.

Rosemary walked carefully down the aisle shifting slightly side-to-side between each row of seats. One hand moved from seat to seat and helped maintain her balance while the other dragged her luggage bag bumping on every row.

"Ms. Howard, please stay safe," the stewardess said with the same brilliant smile.

Rosemary stepped cautiously over the small lip of the aircraft door and onto the stairs. One step at a time she held the rail. She placed her left foot on the next step down, moved her right foot to the same step, then rested her bag on the previous. Each step was a repeat of the last and she moved one step at a time. On the last step, she placed her left foot on the tarmac, gripped the rail, moved her right foot to the ground and rested her bag next to her with its wheels down. Finally, she released her grip from the metal rail, stood straight, and looked at the black horizon. Clouds were thick across the winter sky and no stars could be seen. The only glow was from the overhead lights which illuminated the occasional snowflake and the obvious path to the terminal.

The old woman looked at the boy standing next to her a few feet away. With a warm, loving smile, she said to him, "I'll be alright. It'll be alright."

Erik gave her a faint smile in return, nodded once, then turned to walk to the terminal. Before walking through the door and into the grey building, he looked once more at the old woman now in the distance. Rosemary continued her warm gaze upon him. It was going to be alright.

~

There was little movement inside the building. A middle-aged woman of apparent Hispanic ancestry stood at the sole car rental counter. She was of average height for a Hispanic female but stood tall against the counter. She appeared friendly but empty inside. A void created by the lack of companionship was filled with junk food and television.

A young Native man stood at a podium near the front entrance of the small, remote airport. His blue pleated uniform shirt bore the word **SECURITY** on the back in reflective lettering. He stood at the podium and greeted each traveler as they entered and smiled as each exited. His bright smile contrasted his pale brown skin. His golden eyes complimented his warm smile. His clean-shaven, classy appearance comforted each traveler that he was attentive to details.

An old man with white scruff was sweeping the baggage claim area. His face was bitter with the regrets of his life. He held his wooden broom handle and swept carelessly across the floor. He gave little attention to the patrons of his work area just as the patrons gave little attention to him.

Erik walked through the empty space and exited. Walking toward the traffic circle, he stood under the awning and waited for the city bus which came several times a day. The five mile walk to the city was possible but an uncomfortable trek in the cool winter evening.

In less than an hour from when he landed, Erik got off the city bus in front of the public library and had a short distance to walk. The streets of this small fishing town were partially lit. Old street lamps threw their yellow beams across the broken pavement but the stretch of sidewalk between them was hard to see.

Erik walked the ten blocks from the library to his father's house up the hill. It was a route he was familiar with and needn't light to remind him where to go. As he approached his father's home he remarked, "still hasn't changed." It looked just the same as it had each of the ten years prior.

He lifted the well-worn mat and picked up the corroded key that laid beneath it. He unlocked the door and returned the key to its dark and damp home. Once inside, Erik turned on the living room lights, placed his backpack on the old wool sofa, and kneeled on the unfinished plywood floor in front of the wood stove. His father had been gone for two weeks. The last smoldering ember had long since burned out.

After a few minutes of sitting with his eyes closed, Erik rocked onto his knees, opened the door of the stove and stirred the fluffy, white ash and knocked down fragile structures of dust. He stacked a few pieces of kindling in the firebox, crumpled a page of newspaper and jammed it between the dry sticks. He picked up the box of green safety matches and pulled one out. He struck the match along the side of the box and snapped the match in half. "Damn green matches. Just leave us alone," he cursed to someone not present in the room. After breaking three matches and tossing them in the firebox he got the fourth one to light and touched the burning match to the paper stuffed inside the miniature wooden home. He closed the thick glass door of the wood stove and left the air intake fully open. Wisps of smoke from the paper and wood scraps grew to a column of smoke which escaped from every gap between the stack of kindling slowly catching fire and smoke filled the stove chamber. Erik cracked the door of the stove once again and let in a rush of air sucked in by the draft of the smoldering wood. The growing embers reached a tipping point where the rush of oxygen mixed with the hot gasses and flames gently burst from under the stack of kindling. He closed the stove door again. He continued to watch the small, eager flames lick around the chamber and the once-straight kindling crinkled and bent and began to crack and fall apart. As the kindling fell into a bed of hot coals, Erik grabbed two larger chunks of wood from beside the stove and sat them in front of the stove to wait for their turn in the fire chamber. He put the two pieces of wood on the bed of coals and closed the door once again.

Around the room there was so much to see, even if nothing was different. There were the same childhood pictures on the wall, the same books on the shelf, the same holiday baubles that sat year-round on the window sill, but something felt different. Each year he inspected the items placed around the room but each year he saw something different in them. The laughing and joyful expressions of the family portrait now looked more like a stock image that might have come with the frame.

Erik continued his tour around the room. Between the glowing wood stove and the wool sofa was a bookshelf made from driftwood. A model sailboat in a glass bottle sat on the top shelf just above head-height. Also on the top shelf were a few books with thrift store stickers still on the spine. On the next shelf down, a dozen and a half literary classics were leaning against one another. Steinbeck, Heinlein, Rand, Tolstoy, Solzhenitsyn.

Centuries of human experiences sat untouched on a driftwood plank. The third shelf held photo albums and a history of the family tree, a saga documented by the journals of ancestors who never knew this world. The bottom shelf held staples of every home. An atlas and encyclopedia were stacked flat with another model ship on top of them. Against the sun-bleached driftwood on the bottom of the bookshelf sat two versions of the bible. *How long it has been since these pages saw the light of day,* Erik thought. He picked up the one with a cracked leather binding, blew the dust off the top and flipped through the pages from back to front. A pressed flower fell out of the book as he flipped through the pages and it fell on the floor. "Whoops, let's get you back in there," he said lighthearted. He picked up the dry, violet-colored petals and stem and inspected it for a moment. *Fireweed.* "After a fire clears the forest and leaves nothing but ash and sunlight, you always appear. You prove that beautiful life can always return," he said softly to the preserved flower. Erik carefully placed the flower back on the page it fell off from. He stuck it close to the spine until it stayed in place by itself, then read the first lines directly above it at the top of the page.

Og når jeg fører skyer over jorden, og buen sees i skyen, da vil jeg komme i hu den pakt som er mullem mig og eder og alt levende av alt kjød, og vannet skal aldri mere bli en flom som ødelegger alt kjød.
1 Mosebok 9: 14-15

It shall be, when I bring a cloud over the earth, that the rainbow shall be seen in the cloud; and I will remember My covenant which is between Me and you and every living creature of all flesh; the waters shall never again become a flood to destroy all flesh.
Gen 9:14-15

"Well, God, it's pretty damned cloudy these days," Erik mumbled. He closed the book and placed it back on the bottom of the shelf.

Once the radiant heat from the wood stove began warming the room, Erik adjusted the stove to burn through the night then laid on the wool sofa still in his clothes and covered with a thick blanket. Laying on his side, he observed the fiery show in silence. His mouth did not move as his mind wandered. Scenes from his dreams of the previous night appeared in the flames. The growing flames bent and flickered and rolled against the roof of the chamber desperate to find any crack or hole or opening in which to escape the confines of the black steel box and into the open and free air. The blue and orange flames rose and fell and rose again as the wood shifted and fell apart and shifted again. The chamber of the stove was lined with brick which held the heat and insulated the steel walls. As long as the bricks stayed whole, the steel walls would remain strong and not wear out and last lifetimes. The fire grew hotter and the bricks grew hotter and the steel walls of the stove grew hotter and radiated its heat in waves and began to creak and smell like hot metal as Erik's mind wrestled with the flames confined to the chamber. Even though he stacked new kindling on the dead coals and nursed the embers and gave it new life, the radiant heat of the chamber was now almost too much to bear.

Why did I build this fire? I did not need this fire for comfort as it was chilly inside but it was not too chilly and I was not uncomfortable. I did not need this fire to cook food as there was food available that didn't need cooking. I did not need this fire for light as the electric lights were in order. I built this fire just to watch it burn. I could control this fire. I brought this fire into existence and I could send it right out, again. I could open the stove door and the fire would burn hot and fast and pop embers onto the plywood floor or I could shut the damper and the flames would shrink and shrivel and the embers would dim and die a slow death. I could have not built the fire at all! I controlled this fire. With the damper I can command the flames to rise up, die back, and rise again. Try as I might but I control nothing. I can only control myself and even my own self I cannot control wholly. It was unlikely true control, anyhow.

4

The humid ocean wind is a constant companion to those who live on this rocky isle. Despite the northern latitude, the inhabitants of the Alaskan seas know only one season with slight variation: grey. In summer, the transient sun will make an appearance refreshing the spirits of the land, recharging them and preparing them for the many months of haze and fog that follow. In winter, sea billows roll a frozen fog across the ocean and over the land and through the core of all living things that eke out meager existence on this rock, stranded in seasonal darkness.

Erik woke to the sound of metal flashing slapping the side of the house. The living room window was black. In its reflection was only the red glow of residual embers from the wood stove. He sat up and waited on the edge of the couch allowing the grogginess to pass. He stood and shook the sleep from his legs on the way to the sole bathroom in the house. A plain shag rug in front of the sink covered most of the plywood floor in the small, undecorated room. First letting the water become warm, Erik washed his face and inspected the lingering evidence from two nights prior. His lip was still swollen and the new dark hue outlined his angular jaw against his otherwise pale face. He pulled his phone from his jeans pocket and again took several images. He reviewed them to his satisfaction and felt disgust in his stomach. He showered, changed his clothes, and prepared breakfast.

Shortly after noon, Erik heard steps at the door followed by a key playing in the lock. He stood up in time to see the door open with the wind and a medium height man with short hair and a salty face enter.

"Erik, my son. You have arrived safe. I was not expecting you until the weekend. I am glad to see you but tell me, what is it that caused such a sudden change of plans?" The middle-aged fisherman said with a thick accent.

Erik stepped toward the man and said, "Edward hit me. Mom didn't want to deal with the school again so she sent me here so they wouldn't find out."

His father stood in front of the open door for an extra moment, seeming confused at what he just heard, processing the information. "Oh, I see." He closed the door behind him and turned to take off his boots. He walked to his son standing in the middle of the room and put his hand to Erik's chin. His son turned his head slightly, exposing the bruise that spread across part of his cheek. The fisherman's cold and rough hands felt the heat from the injury, then pulled his son into a tight embrace. "Eg beklagar, min sønn. Eg sviktet deg." *I am sorry, my son. I failed you* he said almost inaudibly. Erik said nothing.

Later, the fisherman prepared a basic supper and asked his son, "would you like to put the tree up? We already have some packages from the family to put under it."

With a half-full mouth, Erik replied, "sure, I guess. The same tree as last year?"

"That is the one. It is in the closet right where you left it."

After finishing the quiet meal, Erik brought the two-piece plastic tree into the living room of the small cabin and placed it in the corner. In a few minutes the job was completed and Erik pulled a large cardboard box from the kitchen across the bare floor. He pulled several packages out of the box. "To: Erik; To: Erik..." He read as he arranged the half-dozen small packages around the tree. The largest package was in a shipping box. He opened it and pulled out two smaller packages wrapped in foreign-looking newspaper. "Erik Larsen," he read on one with a smile. On the other he searched for the tag and read, "Lars Larsen. We both have one, Dad."

"Who is it from?" He called from the kitchen.

"Your sister."

"If it is from Hilde, listen closely for ticking."

Erik laughed and replied, "no, it's from Heidi. She wrapped them just like grandma used to in newspaper."

"She always was the nostalgic one. Always one for tradition, regardless of progress in wrapping paper."

"I always liked grandma and grandpa's packages. I loved reading what was newsworthy in their area three months ago," Erik said pleasantly as he turned his package following the news story across the side and over.

...og uten nærmere forklaring avslo byrådet forespørselen om å blokkere konverteringer av flere byparker til migrantleirer. Kritikere av parkkonverteringene nevner sikkerhetshensyn på grunn av nærliggende barneskoler, men ingen troverdige bevis har blitt lagt frem for de rasistiske påstandene...

...and without further explanation, the counsel rejected the request to block conversion of additional city parks to sanctuary camps for migrants. Critics of the park conversions cite safety concerns near several elementary schools but no credible evidence as been provided regarding the racist claims...

"Uff da," he exhaled as he placed the package with the rest.

"They always did have the best stuff," Lars said as he walked into the living room. He looked at his son sitting on the floor in front of the small Christmas scene. "In fact, they gave you that sweater, ja?"

"Yup. Last year. The last thing they ever sent me." Erik rubbed his fingers over the scratchy wool sweater for a moment. "I always felt like grandma was sending a message with her wrapping paper. Like, she was sending me time. I feel like she was telling me to do something meaningful, newsworthy, something that made a difference. She was giving me the gift of knowledge of time, until she had no more time to give..." His voice trailed off.

"I think she was cheap and didn't want to buy real wrapping paper," Lars laughed.

"You know, Dad, I don't remember them very well. I mean, I can't even remember their voices. I can make out their faces and grandpa's leathery skin. I remember him always wearing his grey wool pants. It could be middle of summer and he wore those same pants. It was ridiculous... And grandma's old lady cheeks. It doesn't seem as funny now but I used to think she looked like a chipmunk with her saggy cheeks."

"I am not surprised you don't remember them very well. You only met them the one time when I moved here," his father replied.

"Yeah... You remember when we went out to dinner that first night? Grandpa Lars couldn't remember how to order in English and asked the lady for a fish drink? She was so confused!" Erik laughed.

"Well, give the guy a break. He hadn't been out of the village for probably thirty years. He was a little rusty." Lars smiled.

"Then he just got so frustrated he started swearing and went to the bar next door. 'En mann kan leve av øl hvis han bærre kan finne kor å få en, fy faen!'" *A man can live on beer if he can just find where to get one, God damnit!* Erik was laughing out loud.

"Ja, ja. Watch your mouth young man. Settle down." Lars sat in his chair for a minute longer and looked to the kitchen. "You know, he wasn't wrong..." He stood, walked to the refrigerator and retrieved a glass bottle.

~

Erik sat on the couch reading old letters from his grandfather while his dad sat in his chair, both facing the wood stove. Erik sat the letter he was reading down and watched at the curling flames through its glass door.

"Dad, what am I going to do about Mom and Edward?" He asked.

His father hesitated for a moment and shifted in his chair. "Eg vet ikkje, Erik *I don't know, Erik.* Eg vet ikkje." He watched the fire for a moment longer and asked back, "why did he hit you?"

"Mom told him I hit her, so he hit me."

"Why did you hit your mother?" Lars asked sharply.

Erik almost jumped. "I didn't hit her! She was chasing me from the house and fell! I didn't even touch her!"

"Why was she chasing you?" He interrogated.

"I skipped school and thought at the park for a while. The school called Mom and when I got back, she was flipping out on me and chased me out of the house! I. Didn't. Touch. Her. Ed hit me!" Erik said exasperated.

"Okay, okay. I believe you." Lars said more calmly. He waited a moment and said, "there are some things in this life you cannot escape. If you listened to you mother she wouldn't chase you out like that. She just wants what is best for you."

"What kind of bullshit is that? She doesn't want what is best for me or she would be doing exactly the opposite of what she is doing." Erik stared at Lars with anger.

"Watch your mouth, boy. You don't talk back to your father like that. That is unacceptable. You should be thankful at Christmas, not making trouble!" Lars said with a snarl.

"Whose side are you on?" Erik exclaimed.

Lars brought his eyebrows down and squinted. "I don't pick sides. I just don't tink you should be giving your mother so much trouble."

Erik closed his eyes, flexed his fingers and toes, released them, looked back and said, "easy for you to say. You left. You couldn't handle her and left me to deal with her by myself."

Lars stood at the accusation and pointed his clubbed finger. "Faen, Erik. Du e min sønn. Eg gjorde det eg måtte for deg!" *Damn you, Erik. You are my son. I did what I had to do for you!*

32

"Du anar ikkje ka som skjer med meg," *You have no idea what is going on with me* Erik softly replied, holding back his pain. He stood from his seat, opened the door, and walked a lonely street until he could hold his emotions no longer.

~

Erik returned to the mariner's cabin long after the winter night fell across the sky. His light brown hair was frosted and his cheeks were pale with rosy centers. Slowly he opened the door, stepped in, and removed his wet shoes.

Lars sat in his chair in front of the stove, also with rosy cheeks. "I was wondering where you went," he said somewhat slurred. "Come here and warm up!"

Erik stepped toward the radiant heat instinctively. Next to his father's chair were a dozen or more empty glass bottles.

The man rose from his chair and patted the boy on his back. "I'm glad you are back! Here, lets get you something to drink to warm up."

He pulled a fresh glass tumbler from on top of the driftwood bookshelf and placed it on the end table pulled close to his chair. He took the tall, clear bottle also sitting on the end table and poured both glasses full. He shoved one into the boy's hands and raised the other, cheering, "skål!" and drank it in one swig. "Akevitt. Norwegian anti-freeze! That will warm even the coldest of men."

Erik looked at the clear fluid in the glass he held and raised it to his lips. Trying to get it all down, he choked on the third sip and coughed some back up. He wiped the Scandinavian liquor off his chin and winced as some of it ran over the split in his lip. Erik placed the glass on the end table and laid down on the couch without saying a word.

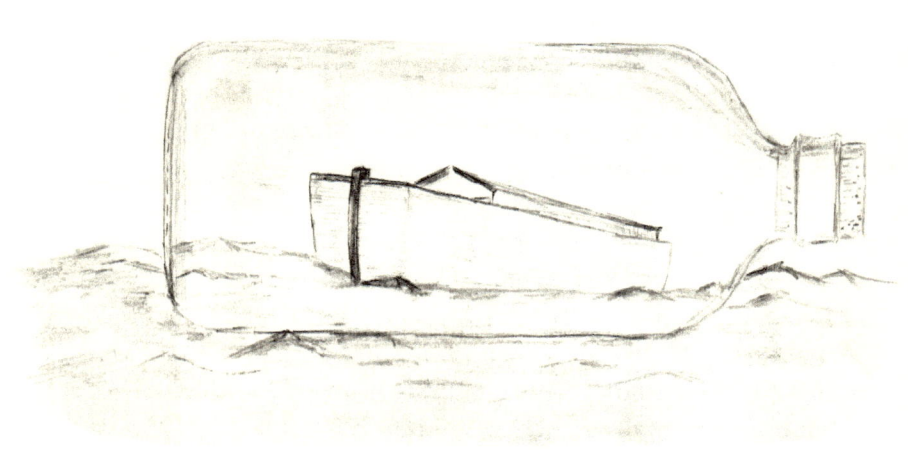

5

School commenced after break.

Erik quietly walked between classrooms avoiding the largest herd of moving people. Crossing in front of a small group clustered around two open lockers, Erik suddenly felt his feet come out from under him. He caught himself in-step and did not fall but looked down to see both of the books he carried on the ground. The group, now behind him, was laughing out loud.

"Dean, that was mean!" A young, brunette girl said. She lightly slapped the jock next to her across his chest.

"Oh come on, Stephanie. He's asking for it!" The biggest of the guys explained to her.

"Yeah, Steph. Just look at the little reindeer fucker. He loves that shit so much he wears it all around school like it's a damn animal pride parade," an older teenage boy said in defense.

"You guys are such jerks," the girl said to them both. She stepped to Erik who was gathering the last of his scattered notes and stuffing them back into random pages of a textbook. She picked up the other book and handed it to him.

"I'm sorry about that, Erik. Don't listen to them. They are just jealous they don't have such a nice sweater as you," Stephanie said to him.

"Ohhh, yeah. We are so jealous of Elfboy Wonder. I mean, what if Rudolph is too stoned to fly tonight! What will we do?!" Dean said waving his bloated arms in the air.

Erik ignored the comment and took the book from Stephanie. "Thanks. Don't worry about it. I take Dean and Carl about as serious as a they take their diet."

"I heard that, Elfboy," Dean lipped back. "If you don't watch out I might trip and fall on you," followed by dramatic gesticulations ending with him falling forward and shoving Erik again.

"Stikk og pul din søster da, taper," Erik said with a petty smirk.

"Uhh, what?" "I don't get it," the two guys said between themselves. "Whatever, man," Dean said before walking away.

"What did you say to them?" Stephanie asked quietly.

Erik replied, "I told him he should find a nice girl, start a family, and settle down in the suburbs."

"No you didn't!" She replied. They both laughed.

"Hey, yo Steph! You comin' Babe or you staying for those Swedish meatballs?" Dean called down the hall, again laughing between his small group.

"Thanks, again. See ya," Erik said before walking the opposite direction.

~

After school Erik sat in a study room of the library skimming through a stack of books he collected. The one holding his attention the longest was a historical journal about the early settlers of the interior of Alaska. Trappers, miners, and other frontiersmen landed on ships at Valdez and walked nearly 400 miles "by shank's mare" taking a month or more to complete the hard traverse.

What would it have been like to grow up in those days? A man could go out and live for himself. He could kill a caribou when he was hungry. He could trap a wolf and collect the bounty when he needed money. Just all alone in the unexplored mountains with nothing but peace and quiet... only his thoughts to keep him company.

"Wouldn't that just be something," Erik said under his breath.

He continued to read a section about the Blackwater Road House and how its owner, Frank Glaser, went on to trap and hunt all over the Alaska range. "For years he stayed out in the wilderness all by himself until he was ready to come out," Erik said to himself. "I wonder what he was hiding from?"

He set the book down with the rest and slid the whole stack into his bag. *Time to get on with it,* he thought.

Erik left the library and walked down the school halls which were nearly empty except for a few remaining people attending after-school groups. Making one last stop to the restrooms, Erik stepped around the corner and relieved himself. Without washing, he started to round the corner back out of the restroom and felt a large object come across his face. He tripped backwards and shouldered into the wall. Dean fell forward into the side-wall carried by his weight after missing the square of Erik's face.

Both boys rebounded and stood at ready to each other with Dean blocking the exit. "You think you can steal Steph right from under me? You little fucker don't know who y'er fuckin' with!" He shouted and threw another punch. Erik was caught just under his eye but moved with the blow to miss most of the force, again. Dean stumbled forward and caught the edge of the sink in his gut. Coughing, he turned and grabbed at Erik's backpack as he was making the corner. Dean's grip on the bag slipped and he fell sideways onto his shoulder. He struggled back up but Erik had run half-way down the hall and well out of range for the winded troll.

Erik ran the mile and a half back to his mother's trailer without stopping. He jumped the steps and onto the plywood porch, almost sliding off the other side over slushy snow. Once inside he quickly kicked his shoes off and walked straight to his room. No one was home.

In the bathroom he looked at himself and assessed the damage. "Just a little abrasion," he said quietly while dabbing his wound with a damp washcloth.

Back to his room, Erik continued flipping through his stack of library books until Bethany returned from her shift late in the evening.

"Hi, sweetie. How was school today? Did you learn anything?" She asked with an unlit cigarette clenched between her teeth. She fumbled with a lighter while setting her jacket on the kitchen counter.

"I found some cool books. So, I guess that's something," he replied while opening the fridge.

"Oh yeah? What kind of books?" She inhaled deeply and let out a stream of smoke toward the ceiling.

"I dunno. Just about the trappers and settlers," Erik replied.

"Well, don't get any bright ideas. Those days are long gone. Looong gone," she said staring through the wall.

Erik went back to his room and sat on his bed reading through the night.

~

The following day, Erik had just sat down at his desk before the teacher called him up.

"Erik, you are wanted in the principle's office," the middle-aged lady said with a monotone.

"Why?" Erik asked in reply.

"I don't know. They just called for you and said you were wanted," she said uninterested.

Erik walked through the office door and saw a large blob of a man with a hurt scowl in the corner and the principle standing next to him. The old Latina woman looked at Erik with her hands on her hips, her waist strained her pantsuit. "Mr. Larsen, this young man said you tried to corner him in the men's bathroom last night after school. What do you have to say for yourself?"

"Uhh, what?" Erik said somewhat shocked and confused.

"You heard me. I have a credible accusation of bullying on your part and I want to hear your side of the story. Mr. Garcia claims you hit him and pushed him over. He has an injured shoulder to prove it," the woman said with a serious voice.

"What? Dean punched me!" He pointed to the small abrasion high on his cheekbone. "He tried to ambush me and fell as I ran away. I didn't touch him once."

"Then why didn't you report the incident as soon as you could? Why would Mr. Garcia report his own bullying?" The woman said now waving one hand.

Erik looked between the swollen administrator and her male prodigy sitting on a chair holding his shoulder. It was obvious to Erik the bloated kid was baring down, forcing wetness into his eyes. "If I had reported it, would you have believed me?"

"Mr. Larsen, I don't know what to believe. Especially with your recent track record of mischief, I hesitate to take your account as gospel."

"Uh huh. And how about Dean's track record?" Erik asked curiously.

"Mr. Garcia has been an upstanding student and athlete. You might actually learn something from hi..."

Erik interrupted, "do you really believe that I tried to pick a fight with Dean? I am 120-pounds. He's practically twice my weight..." Erik looked back to Dean, down to Dean's feet, then back up to the lady, "...or more. Why in the world would I get anywhere near him? I'll tell you, there is no reason. Not one damned reason I give any care to this kid. He is a jerk and a bully and torments everyone around him, and I am sorry for him." He continued without giving a chance for interruption. "I am truly sorry for Dean and whatever shit he has going on at home. The kind of tormenting he must have under his roof is probably twice as bad as what he takes out on me and everyone else. Dean, I don't know what it is like at home for you but I am genuinely, deeply sorry. It isn't your fault. None of it. But taking it out on me and manipulating figures of authority are not going to free you. This will eat at you from the inside out and you'll have nothing to show for it at the end of the day except a miserable, worthless existence. Bullying me will not fix your problems. Women may 'find themselves' but men 'make themselves.' And what you are making yourself into is a goddamn disgrace and waste of a human. Ms. Corcoran is right, you could be an upstanding guy if you stop bringing your problems with you to school and wearing them around your neck. You are an aging child right now and I know that sounds harsh, and it is harsh, and I am in a lot of the same shit you are, but there are some things in life you cannot escape: you cannot escape yourself. So at the end of this day, are you going to make yourself into someone you like? Someone you feel responsible for? Or are you going to keep dragging your knuckles along and blaming everyone else for your problems?" Erik finished with a deep breath and stared at Dean sitting speechless with a confused look on his face.

"You, you can't talk to this boy like that," the principle finally sputtered. "I ought to have you disciplined for being so mean!"

"No. You should be disciplined for being so mean and lying to him. I am the only one that has probably ever been nice, actually nice and giving him the hard truth. Good day." Erik turned and left the room before either person could respond.

A few hours later a note was delivered to Erik's last class: a detention slip for the next day to be signed by a parent or guardian.

~

"Erik, what is this on the counter?" Bethany called across the house. Erik sat on his bed cross-legged with a book in his lap. He gently closed the book and walked into the kitchen.

"I have to stay for detention tomorrow. I talked-back to the principle," he said plainly.

"What is wrong with you? Skipping class, running off, disrespecting the authorities?" She said waving the detention form in his face.

"She was wrong. She wa..."

Bethany interrupted, now irate. "Erik, when will you learn that the teacher is right? How many times are you going to tell me some story about 'you are right' and 'everyone else is wrong' when we both know you are lying. What is going on in that head of yours?"

"Mom. She was wrong. I was right." He said slowly.

"That is exactly what I mean. When are you going to stop lying to me!" She called hysterically.

Erik turned and walked back to his room closing the door in the woman's face behind him. She pushed the door and slammed it into the wall and stomped to his bed where he sat down. "Is this it? You are reading all these stories about the wild west and you think you can be some kind of cowboy?"

He looked at her with a genuinely confused face.

"Answer me, damnit!" She yelled.

"What the hell is goin' on in here, slammin' the door an' yellin'? What'd the little shit do now?" Ed called loudly as he entered the room, still groggy from sleeping on the couch.

"Ed, Erik got detention and is trying to lie to me about it," she said back to him. Erik sat on his bed looking straight and ignoring both of them.

"Ahh, is that right? What a little shit." Ed picked up the three books on the bed and looked at the covers. "Is this it? You readin' about fairy tales and think you are some character gettin' to make up the rules as you go along? What horseshit," he said as he held the front and rear cover of the biggest book and started to pull it apart.

"What are you doing?!" Erik cried. "Those are from the library! What the fuck!" Erik watched the grotesque man grunt as he ripped pages from one book and tore the cover off another.

"There!" He said as he threw them at the garbage can. "Now get that shit outta here and don't bring it back, you hear me!"

Erik sat on his bed, speechless, his eyes getting red.

"I say 'you hear me'?" The man said again with spittle over Erik's face.

"Yeah," Erik mouthed.

Ed walked to the door behind Bethany, "that shit," pointing at Erik, "that shit, will not happen again in this house."

Bethany stepped to the bed and looked at the boy. "Well, you heard the man. Now knock it off."

~

Bang! The door burst open. Erik woke with panic and reached for his lamp pushing it off the end table. Footsteps neared him until a bright light from the ceiling blinded him temporarily and made him wince. The man and woman were grabbing at Erik, throwing the sheets off his near naked body jolting him upward. "Whaaah?!" He sounded as he was dragged by his leg to the edge of the bed.

"Stop it! Stop moving!" Ed shouted as he tried to hold down Erik's arms. Bethany stood to his side and ripped a few feet of duct tape off the roll. She tried to wrap it around the boy's wrists but the tape got tangled and stuck to itself while he fought.

"Hold still damn you!" The woman shrieked.

"Get off, get off me," Erik grunted as he pulled his arms out from the man's sweaty grip. The odor of alcohol and nicotine poured off the man. "Let...go!"

"We are just trying to help you! You are not well, Erik! You need to see someone right now!" Bethany yelled.

Erik got one hand free again and punched at Ed. Ed rolled to his side and landed on the bed and struggled to get back upright. Erik jumped to the head of the bed and stood on it pushing his back against the wall. "Get out! Get out of here!" He exclaimed.

Ed fell off the bed in his struggle and hit his head on the bed frame. Semi-conscious he raised himself and crashed wall-to-wall until he found his route out of the room, eventually falling on his bed in the adjacent room. Bethany, now without backup, hesitated a moment before backing out of the room and slamming her bedroom door. Erik jumped off his bed, closed his door and pushed the button lock on the handle. He put his back to the door, slid down until he sat on the floor and panted. Once he was sure Ed was passed out, he dressed himself, put on a dark jacket, and quietly dropped out the window.

~

"Hallaien? Erik? Do you have any idea what time it is?" A muffled voice said on the other end of the line.

"Yeah, I know what time it is! Mom and Ed just tried to tie me up. I'm just walking around and I don't know what's going on Dad. Fuck. I don't know what to do," he said choked up.

"Wha? Tie you up? What does that even mean? Where are you?" Lars said confused.

"She knocked down my door and tried to tape me while Ed held my arms. I don't know what is going on!" Erik said almost in tears.

"Alright, alright. Calm down. Where are you?"

"I don't know. Uhh, somewhere on Muldoon? I think? Fuck. Dad. I don't know. It's snowing. It's dark. I don't have any clue."

"Are you guys fighting again or something?" The man said slightly more alert.

"No, Dad. I just thought I'd go for an evening stroll in the middle of a goddamn blizzard at three in the morning for shits and giggles!"

"I'm just trying to help, Erik. Stop with the sarcasm. What are you arguing about that is so damned important it's worth running away for?" He asked irritated.

"Mom is going off the deep end, Dad. I...I...can't handle her anymore. I can't do it. I can't...fucking do it!"

"Maybe if you stopped arguing with her so much she wouldn't get so upset?"

"What?! Are you fucking drunk? She is insane! She tried to tie me up with duct tape and take me to some fucking institution in the middle of the night!" Erik gasped between his words.

"What are you saying? I'm not a goddamn drunk and I am getting real tired of you not respecting your parents. Maybe you should walk those streets until your little feet freeze off and you start to see how much your parents are giving up so you can have a decent fucking life!" Erik winced and held the phone away from his ear.

He held the phone in front of his face and yelled at the lit screen, "Faen ta deg! You don't give a flying fuck about me! You didn't care about me when you ran off and you don't care about me now. I called you for help and all you do is tell me what a worthless piece of shit I am. Maybe it's you that's the worthless piece of shit! What did I do to deserve this! My mom is batshit insane and my dad is fucking gone! Who do I have? Fucking nobody. Not a fucking person in this fucking world cares what happens to me! Fuck you and fucking forget about me!"

Erik slapped the screen with his thumb until the phone went black and he squeezed its plastic case until his hand hurt. He squatted to his hams and hung his head down, holding his agony. His heart pounded. His head pounded. His gut wrenched.

6

Erik knew not what laid behind the door. He stood in front of the entrance for several minutes that morning, shivering and sleepless. Though cold, tired, and tormented, Erik knew what he must do. Standing still was not it.

He turned the knob. It was unlocked. He opened the door and stepped in. Nobody was in the living room. He stepped inside closing the door quietly behind him, and took one light step after another toward his room without removing his shoes. He rounded the corner to his bedroom and stood at the door frame, paused. The pale, ghostly woman was sitting in the folding chair at his small desk smoking a cigarette. A menthol haze surrounded her as she stamped out the glowing end and dropped the butt on top of several others. Ash settled across the scattered papers. *Okay. Here goes nothing.*

"Mom, I have something I want to say," Erik said, obviously uncomfortable. The woman looked at him.

"Mom, I want to apologize for last night. You were right. I was wrong. I have been out of my mind and not thankful for all the work you are doing holding this house together. That's... that is why I decided I am going to get my act together and straighten myself out. I am going to take school serious. And, and I am going to get a job after school and start pulling my own weight around here. It's time I take some responsibility for my actions." Erik stood upright and now more confident even though his voice still had a tremble from the restrained shivers.

Lighting a cigarette, she continued her distant stare. "Good."

~

The bus route from the high school to downtown did not take long. Erik walked passed the strip of diners, bars, gift shops, and other businesses looking for help. Once at the end of the business district, Erik turned around and walked back. First on his mental list was a generic sporting goods store. He entered the business and went to the customer service desk.

"Excuse me ma'am. I was wondering if you know if you guys are hiring anyone right now?" He asked uncertain.

"Oh, uhh. I am not sure. Maybe. You can go to our website and look there. Here's the website," she said handing him a business card.

"Okay. Thank you." Erik turned and left.

Next down the row of potential, preferable employers was a chain-owned outdoor recreation retailer. He found the same unhelpful response from the person at customer service and repeated the experience three more times before stopping and sitting on a frosty bench at the bus stop. It was only mid-afternoon but was beyond dusk in the northern city. Erik sat on the lip of the bench trying to reduce his contact with the cold cement seat. His jeans wicked the melting crust where he sat.

He watched a few people walk by on the other side of the street. Thinking of his next plan, he saw a grizzled old man with a respectable beard come out of a business with few signs in the window.

"Huh. I didn't notice that place before. Kind of a hole-in-the-wall between the other shops," he said, squinting to read the letters on the door. Erik stood and crossed the middle of the street between traffic.

Great North Trapping, Co.

Under the bold typeface read:

Fur Buyer – Supplies – Clothing

In smaller print:

Peddlers Turn Around

Erik opened the door and warm air billowed across his face carrying a sweet aroma of pipe tobacco and burning wood. Inside he saw several racks of skins and pelts and furs of all kinds of creatures. The room was larger than it appeared on the outside but still small compared to the corporate floor plans. Across the room he saw an old man sitting in a leather chair flipping pages of an unfamiliar magazine. The old man looked up at the boy. He cleared his throat and said with a deep, gruff voice, "can I help you, son?"

After one moment too long, Erik broke the awkward silence with a quiet, "I was wondering if you were hiring anyone right now?"

The man turned his head and said, "you're gunna hafta speak up, son. What do you need?"

More clearly he said, "I am looking for a job. Are you hiring?"

"Looking for a job, you say? Come over here and close the door, will you? You're letting all the cold in." The grizzled man worked his way up and stood at the wood counter at the back of the showroom. He straighten his leather vest and pulled his tin pants up a little higher by its belt. "Come over here and let's talk."

Erik approached, trying to not get distracted by the items hanging around him. "Yes, sir. I am looking for a job," he said with an uncertain smile.

"Well, what can you do?" The man replied plainly.

"Uhh, I am not sure. I have never worked before. I guess I don't really have any skills," Erik replied. Embarrassment crept to his face.

"Then why, by God, should I hire you to do nothing?" The old man frowned.

"Ohh, well, I can learn pretty fast. I, I don't know very much about any of this," he turned and softly gestured to the showroom, "but I would sure like to, mister."

"You say you 'don't know very much', well, how much, exactly, do you know about this business?"

Erik paused for a moment and looked between the old man's serious expression and a painting of a cabin behind him. "I... I guess I don't know anything, really." He paused for another second and added, "but I will show up on-time and I won't complain!"

"What is your name?" The man asked, now leaning on his arms over the varnished counter.

"My name is Erik, sir. Erik Larsen."

"What do you want to learn, Erik?"

"I don't know what there is to learn. I don't know enough about it. I know I have read a lot of books about the old trappers and the gold rush and the Russian settlers and traders."

"You know they write about that stuff real romantic like. It sure wasn't all fun and games back then. No roads, colder winters, no medicine. You always read about the folks that made it big but not about the thousands of others that died from starvation because they missed the migration or couldn't find the trail."

Erik replied quickly, "I understand that, sir. I am not out to be some high-and-mighty trapper legend. I just need a job and would rather do something I am interested in."

"First jobs suck, kid. Most kids never get a choice. Hell, my first job was shoveling coal into buckets for twelve hours a day, and I still had to get my school work done."

"Listen, mister. I need a job. Do you have a job available? I can do whatever you need. I won't complain. I'll show up when you tell me. If I don't know how, I'll learn it on my own time. But if you aren't hiring then I need to move along and find someone who is," Erik replied smartly.

The old man looked at the boy for a moment longer. "Okay. Tell you what. I appreciate you having the balls to come in here and ask for what you want. There hasn't been a kid do that in here for a decade. Asking for what you want is a lost art and I respect that. Why don't you come in tomorrow and we'll try you out for a day and see what you can do. I'm sure I can find something here for you. Are you in school? What time can you be here?"

"Oh, uhh, thank you, sir. Yeah, uh, yes I am in school. I can be here by, uh... 3:30 and all day on the weekends!" Erik stuttered in surprise.

"Okay. Be here at 3:30 tomorrow. We close at 6. That will give you a couple hours to try things out. Pay is minimum until I figure out if you can work or not."

"Oh, gosh. Thank you, sir. I'll be ready!"

"Right, and enough with the 'sir' stuff. You can call me Bill."

"Thank you, Bill. I'll be here at 3:30." Erik held his hand out to meet Bill's and shook it firmly. He turned around and bumped into the rack behind him and knocked off a fox pelt. He picked it up and hung it back on the rack. He walked more carefully to the door, turned and again said, "thanks, uhh, thank you... Bill."

The following day inched along. As soon as the final bell rang, Erik walked quickly down the halls and outside. He ran for the bus stop a few blocks away on the downtown route. There he sat for twenty minutes composing himself for his first day at work.

~

Three minutes before his decided time, Erik entered the classy and rugged frontiersman's shop.

"Ahhah. I wasn't sure you'd show," Bill said from behind the counter. An equally grizzled man with slightly more grey in his beard was standing next to him with his back to Erik. The other man turned to see who Bill was speaking to.

"Oh, is this the boy you were tellin' bout?" The man's voice was deep and course like a lifelong smoker's voice.

"Yeah, that's him alright," Bill replied with a smile.

"Yes, sir. I am here right on time and ready for anything," Erik said.

The old men both laughed to each other. Bill looked back to Erik and said, "well, how about you just start with cleaning the place up a bit. Everything you need is in that closet over there. You ain't above cleaning work are you?" Bill asked with a peculiar tone.

"Oh, no. I'll get right to it." Erik set his bag in the small closet, pulled out a broom and dust pan and commenced sweeping. The old men ignored the boy and resumed their conversation.

"Well, Bill, I think there's enough hot air in this dump now the kid might pass out. Good seein' ya."

"Thanks for comin' by, Joe. Give Dawn my best," Bill replied.

"Will do," Joe said. He turned and walked toward the door. He said to Erik in passing, "you don't let this slave driver here ride you too hard, now." He was out the door before Erik thought of something to say.

Closing time approached. Bill shut off the register and made notes in a log book. After his paperwork was complete, he put his glasses on the counter and looked up at Erik as he was polishing the metal racks. "Erik," he said.

"Erik," he said a little louder.

"Oh, yes Bill?" He replied.

"It is 6 o'clock. You did a good job today. The place looks sharper than it has in a long time, but don't let it get to your head. Why don't you put it up for the night and come back tomorrow. I'll take you every day after school. In two weeks probation we'll renegotiate your salary and see if you are a one-day-wonder or if you stick to it. Can you do that?"

Erik looked thrilled. "Absolutely. Monday to Friday, same time. Thank you, sir."

The next day, Friday, was similar and he continued cleaning where he left off. Erik was wholly compliant at home that weekend and had little trouble, eager for Monday to arrive.

~

"Well, Erik, I must say you have done a fine job. I suppose I should probably find something new for you to work on before you buff a hole right through the floor," Bill said Monday afternoon.

"Just tell me what you need and I'll do it," Erik replied.

The old man looked thoughtful for a moment. He stood from the counter and walked to the front of the room, watching people walk by the glass windows. "Come here, Erik. Let's walk around and I'll show you all we have here."

"Do you know what animals these are?" Bill pointed to an assorted rack.

Erik looked and felt several specimens. "This is a hare. This is a fox, of course. I guess this is a... marten? I don't know."

"That is a beaver. You feel the wool under the guard hairs, here? They don't grow in a direction. That's what makes beaver fur so soft," Bill described as he was rubbing a pelt. "Do you have any experience with trapping or know anyone who traps?"

"No. Only what I've read about in books. I think my grandpa trapped when he was younger but he's dead," Erik replied.

"Is this a trade you want to learn?"

"Maybe. I don't know. I hear it isn't the same kind of business as it once was but some guys still make it work."

"Yes, some guys are still running lines but it is a hard job. It can be a fun hobby if you know what you're doin' but it's a tough haul," Bill said shaking his head.

Erik looked at the rack of wolf skins and petted the scruff.

Bill noted Erik's sentimental posture. "Now, you ain't one of these environmental types that is going to clean me out and burn down the store are you?"

Erik pulled his hand back and looked straight to Bill, wide eyed. "God, no! I was just admiring the fur was all."

Bill chuckled. "Okay. Don't worry, I believe you. You ain't the type. Those punks come in with their heads all shaved funny and too many hair colors not known to man. The girls are runnin' around usin' their bodies like a frat house mattress and the boys all have so much goddamn hardware in their faces they probably get NPR on-demand." Bill chucked at his next thought, "heh, maybe that's exactly their problem? They spend all their time listening to what people tell them to think and not half a second thinking for their own selves."

"That's how I feel sometimes..." Erik said dourly.

"I get the feeling you aren't like that, Erik. Why are you different than those punks always giving me grief and painting over my windows?"

"I don't know. I don't feel different. I just feel like me, like Erik. I feel like I don't fit in, that's for sure. I don't have many friends. Well, none really..." Erik looked down, then across the room. He took a deep breath as though garnering something resembling courage. "I have always wondered if I am the normal one and everyone else is crazy, but then it comes to me that it's more likely that I am the crazy one and everyone else is normal. I don't know, Bill. I don't know why I'm different. Sometimes I wish I wasn't." Erik stood on his toes and stretched his calves, then rested flatfooted again. "Seems like all of my peers are explicitly trying to 'be different' but the funny thing is, they all just end up looking and acting the same. I am just trying to get by and I am the one that turns out different."

"I see," the old man said. "I can assure you that all of your generation is pretty much gone crazy. It isn't you," he said again with a frown.

After a moment of mutual self-reflection, Bill continued to show Erik around the floor. He introduced the boy to all the different creatures that hung on the wall. Skins and pelts, knives and ulus. Bone needles and sinew. The old man showed each kind of trap he carried in the store, traditional and modern variants. Each model and each size had a specific task it was built to perform.

"Do you have a good pair of mittens?" Bill asked.

"I have some just regular snow gloves. Nothing special but they work."

"No, those won't do. Here, why don't you take this home." Bill took a home-wrapped package off the shelf. "My wife started making these kits. They're meant as a fun project for kids to get into the trade. There are two muskrat pelts in there with instructions on how to size your hands and trace on the skins. It has a razor, a pack of needles and some fake sinew. All you need is a pen to trace with. Why don't you take this one here home and make yourself a pair of mittens and we'll see how you do. If you do half-decent maybe I'll start showing you how to grade the furs I'm buying."

Erik stood flabbergasted. "I, Bill, this is expensive. I can't pay for this."

"It is far from the most expensive thing in the store. Now, I'll make you a deal. This one is a gift. You get a discount on anything you want to buy in the future but this one is on me. I just hope I'm not gettin' soft in my old age and losing my good sense, but I think you'll actually appreciate it."

"I certainly do. I don't know what to say," Erik said, almost embarrassed.

"How about 'thank you' and just work on it when you have the time. I'll be happy to see what you come up with."

"Thank you, Bill. I'll start on it tonight."

"You are welcome. Old people like helping young people they think are worth it. The problem is, there ain't hardly noone worth it any more. Alright. Time to close up. I'll quiz you tomorrow on the traps. It's important you get those figured out first in case someone asks you about 'em.'"

"Okay. I'll see you tomorrow. Thanks again." Erik grabbed his backpack from the broom closet and left to catch the evening bus.

~

Erik sat on his bed and rested the gift on his lap. He gently peeled the seams back but still tore the brown paper where the tape was stuck to it. Inside the package was a complete do-it-yourself kit, all of its components carefully selected by masculine ruggedness and feminine detail. It was the perfect gift for any aspiring woodsman or homemaker. He removed two muskrat pelts and felt the soft flow of its fur and the grain of its skin. He brushed one against his cheek and goosebumps raised on the back of his neck. He held it to his face and admired the natural leather smell. Below the pelts was a small paper bag. Its contents: a pack of three heavy plastic needles, a roll of thick plastic thread, a cardboard-covered razor blade, and a piece of paper folded in quarters. Erik unfolded the paper and read:

To him who has the conviction to love others,
    to Him love shall be given.
To him who has the desire to love himself,
    to him the earth shall be given.
Please bless this creature that gave its life, for it is the life of this small and insignificant creature that sustains us.

So God created man in His own image; in the image of God He created him; male and female He created them. Then God blessed them, and God said to them, "Be fruitful and multiply; fill the earth and subdue it; have dominion over the fish of the sea, over the birds of the air, and over every living thing that moves on the earth." Then God saw everything that He had made, and indeed it was very good. Gen 1:27-28, 31

The opposite side of the page read directions guiding the proper shape, sizing, and construction of the custom, home-made mittens. Erik read the directions several times and began sizing his hands on each pelt.

As he roughly traced his left hand with a pen, Erik stopped and looked up at his swinging door. It was now open and an ogre stood in the frame.

"Hey, there. Whatcha got going on there squirt?" Ed slurred. He approached the bed with a stagger and picked up one pelt.

"Nothing. Just working on a school project," Erik replied without looking up.

"A proj-eckt school, eh? I don't 'member play'n with no dead cats 'n school. Guess they must' got a new teacher now." The odor pouring off the sweaty man was putrid. "Well now we should jus' put these kitties right where they be'long."

Ed grabbed the pelt and the box and ineffectively roughed them up, throwing them on the ground. Erik sat, confused by the tantrum.

"Now think you twice 'fore bring dead cats in this here home. This's a special place." Spit rained on Erik's head. He continued to sit still.

"And I have something real special-like to give that special lad'ee in that room right there." Ed's hand waved toward the window.

Ed stood as straight as could be in his condition and crashed from wall to door until he made it into the hall. He crashed his own bedroom door open and called to the unseen woman on the bed, "hey there girl. Ol' Ed's got somethin' special for you'u'u."

"Ed! I am trying to sleep! What the hell are you doing?" Bethany shouted through the wall.

"Oh, come now girl. Jus' give me a little chance! I don't wan' much."

Erik heard what sounded like wrestling on the bed and a modest struggle.

"Come now Beth! I jus' want a little!" He said more forcefully.

"Stop it! Get off! Get off of me!" The woman called.

"Damnit, hold still!"

The muffled words weren't hard to make out. Erik could imagine everything plain as day through the thin trailer walls. After a moment more of grunting and struggling, Erik was sure their focus was off of him. He walked as silent as possible to his bedroom door, turned the knob, and closed it. It didn't help much, but it helped enough.

Back on his bed, Erik turned his room light off and put on a small headlamp. From the dim light he continued his work on the wrinkled pelt through the night until his work was completed.

~

"Look at what I came up with, Bill!" Erik called as he entered the store. He held up two lumpy mittens, one on each hand.

The old man looked up from his magazine and over his glasses at the excited boy. "Why, isn't that something? Let me take a look at those and see how you done." He reviewed them for a full minute.

"Upon close inspection, it is with great pride that I place my seal of approval. Of course, there is lots of room for improvement, but that comes with time and practice. Good going, Erik. You did a good job on these seems here," Bill said with a great smile through his beard. His wrinkles stretched on his face.

"Thank you, Bill. I stayed up all night putting it together!"

"Well, now Erik. I don't want to hear you start slipping in school on account of home crafts."

"Are you kidding? I get more education here with you in the shop in a day than I get in a whole year in that jail." They both laughed at the truth of his statement.

"Today is going to be an exciting day. I just got a call earlier from an old friend. He says he was in the gold this last month and is going to give me first pick of the catch. He should be in around closing time and we'll negotiate. Until then, how's about you get things tidied up and then I'll start showing you what to look for before he gets here."

"Alright. That sounds exciting!"

Once the shelves were straightened, pelts hung and spaced on the rack, and the floor swept, Erik came up to Bill who was inspecting several wolf pelts laying on the counter.

"Okay, now, Erik. You see this one here? This is a prime specimen. It is perfect. We are looking for nicks in the skin where the knife poked too deep. We are looking here on the paws and the snout, and any holes from where the trapper dispatched the animal." Erik followed Bill's lecture with his hand, feeling the descriptions. "And this here, this is a bad one. There are scuffs and nicks ever'where. The paws were cut off at the ankles. And see here? It looks like the man used a goddamn cannon on this critter! Just a little bitty .22 caliber will do just fine. You see, when the animal is in the trap, it doesn't have anywhere to go. Most of the time they stand still and try to size you up. It is your job as the trapper to dispatch the critter as humanely as possible but also to make the most use of their fur. It is all about waste. We take these creatures from the earth. The least we can do is make the most use possible from them and make it mean something."

"Just like my mittens," Erik acknowledged.

"That's right. Just like those mittens of yours," Bill said in confirmation.

"Now, this one here in the middle, it is what you'll see from an experienced amateur. This guy here, he is getting fast but he still hasn't figured out the tricks."

"What do you mean? 'The tricks?'" Erik asked.

"Yeah, 'the tricks.' The little details you only learn from old geezers who've been around the block a few times. This here wolf came from a trapper who's a kid a bit older than you. I think this is his seventh season on the line. Anyway, he is getting cocky because he can skin a wolf as fast as any of the old-timers but he isn't as good. You can see that here," he pointed to a wave along the edge.

"This fella, he is all balls and no brain and don't take advice from no one. So, we stopped giving it to him. Every time he comes in with a new stack of pelts to sell, I grade them and give him the middle price. He says they're worth top-grade and takes them down the street. That guy gives him low-grade and he comes right back asking if our deal is still good! Well, I try to tell him how to get to top-grade but he doesn't seem all that interested. He says he knows what he's doing and I'm just cheatin' him. So, I just stopped trying and so did everyone else. Kid's young, dumb, and full'a… uhh, spunk," Bill finished looking a little embarrassed.

Erik stifled his giggling but let a few chuckles out at the old man's faux pas. "It doesn't seem that hard once you know what to look for."

"No it ain't. It is easy work or I wouldn't still be doing it here. I'd be locked in some government-run nursing home, otherwise. It's easy stuff, you just need to get the hang of it, kid. You're as sharp as a tack. You'll pick it up in no time if you don't start gettin' cocky on me."

Erik inspected the three specimens closely moving from one to the other, comparing each detail to the rest. He also took a few hare pelts from the bargain bin and inspected them. A few minutes later a man opened the door and walked inside with a large tote in tow.

"Hey, Paul, how the hell are ya?" Bill called from across the room.

Erik had already walked toward the visitor. "Hello, sir. Can I help carry your tote?"

The short, squatty man pulled his hood back to better look at the unfamiliar boy and was confused. "Huh? Hey, Bill, who's this guy?"

"Paul, this is Erik. He's helping me out in the afternoons. Go on, Erik. Go ahead and wheel that tote over by the counter. We'll unload 'er in a minute."

Paul lightened and changed his tone. "How 'ya doin' Erik. You payin' off some gamblin' debt to this geezer? He cheats, I swear it's true!" He said with a great belly laugh.

Bill joined with a self-incriminating chuckle. "I don't have to cheat with you, Paul. You wouldn't know a good crib if it kicked you in the shorts."

"Kid," Paul said to Erik, "you want a real kick in the shorts you have Bill's old lady cook you supper some time. That'll put hair on your balls!"

"Yeah, yeah. It's better now that she doesn't use the mutt as a taste-tester," Bill replied with a pat of his belly.

Erik was almost in tears trying to stifle his laughter.

"Okay, Paul. What you got for me this time?" Bill asked removing the lid from the plastic tote.

"How's about six wolf, four grey and two black. Three fox. And two dozen marten," Paul said proudly.

"Two dozen marten? You're going to start a bank run with numbers like that. They've sure been strong this year, haven't they?" Bill replied, pleasantly surprised.

The old man inspected two marten pelts quickly. "Okay, Erik. Take a look at these and tell me which one is better or if either are any good."

Erik inspected both specimens. "This one here has a rougher-looking spot at the base of the neck. It's kind of hard to see but I can feel it. This other one doesn't have that but the tail doesn't lay flat. They both are better looking than anything in the bargain bin, that's for sure."

Bill smiled. "That's a good answer. Paul here is an expert. If you were to tell him his stuff looked like the scraps in the bin then you might just find yourself taking ten paces." Both men smiled and laughed.

"But, that doesn't mean he is perfect. Just like that rough spot, there. It isn't a deal breaker but it does matter when grading these. I wasn't sure you'd pick up on it."

Bill continued to look at each pelt, then gave it to Erik who accurately described what he saw and what he felt.

"Well, Paul. This all looks good to me," Bill said.

The two men negotiated for a while and Erik stood to the side and observed. He listened to their words, their expressions, their tones. He watched the body language of each man as they haggled over the dollar figure of each item. When the deal was complete, both men shook hands.

"Good deal. Thanks for coming in, Paul."

"No problem, Bill. You know, you don't have to be a stranger. Why don't you come out to my place one of these days. Maybe you could con this boy into tagging along. Might do him some good being around a few crackpots like ourselves," Paul said as he buttoned up his jacket.

Bill leaned on the counter and raised one eyebrow. "What are you trying to tell me, Paul?"

"You knows exactly what I mean. Don't work this kid too hard." And then he was gone, lost among the people shuffling by.

"What he was saying is right, Erik. You do have an eye for this. Do you have any interest in learning the trap line?"

Erik looked at the man and considered the meaning of what Bill asked. He spoke carefully, considering each word, "there are few things I can look forward to besides what I could learn from people like you."

The two men looked at each other for a moment. Erik was the first to break eye contact and started stacking the newly purchased inventory.

"Well... tell you what. We are almost done with the season this year. Marten closed end of February and not a lot of what's left is in good shape. This load of Paul's was probably his last paycheck for the winter. So, let's spend the next few months teaching you more the ins and outs of all the different styles of traps we use, do some homework on your own, and by next winter you'll be just as ready as can be. This summer when things is getting dried out and you're out of school, we can take a field trip and I'll show you how to put these things out. It won't be quite the same but it'll put some practice to what you're readin' in the books."

"Bill, that's an incredible thought. I, I'm grateful for the offer!" Erik replied, obviously excited.

"It looks like you'll be sticking around here a little while. How about we talk about store benefits. How's about I'll give you half-off one piece of equipment a month and you can pay it off in weekly installments deducted from your paycheck. That way you can start picking things up slowly, maybe we'll have some sales you can take advantage of. Then by next winter you'll have your own cache of equipment to set up. I bet we can probably find a guy who isn't using part of his line and you can try running it on the weekends."

"That's just... thank you."

Bill walked to a shelf with an assortment of metal jaws, chains, and other implements. He picked a rectangular hoop off a display hanger and walked back to Erik. He set the tool on a clear spot of the counter. "Here. This is a 110 conibear, we call it. This is an all 'round general purpose trap for small furbearers, big enough for marten but won't cream a mink or other little critter. You can even practice with squirrels. Take this home and start playing with it. It won't bite your finger off but I wouldn't snap myself for fun. Just grab a few sticks and start gettin' the hang of setting it and see how much pressure it takes to snap. We'll deduct the cost of it out of your next few checks at that discounted rate. That outta hold your enthusiasm for a while."

✝

Q

Keep thy heart with all diligence;
for out of it are the issues of life.
Proverbs 4:23 KJV

Praise the Lord!
 Blessed is the man who fears the Lord,
Who delights greatly in His commandments.
 His descendants will be mighty on earth;
 The generation of the upright will be blessed.
Wealth and riches will be in his house,
And his righteousness endures forever.
Unto the upright there arises light in the darkness;
He is gracious, and full of compassion, and righteous.
 A good man deals graciously and lends;
 He will guide his affairs with discretion.
 Surely he will never be shaken;
 The righteous will be in everlasting remembrance.
 He will not be afraid of evil tidings;
 His heart is steadfast, trusting in the Lord.
His heart is established;
He will not be afraid,
Until he sees his desire upon his enemies.
 He has dispersed abroad,
 He has given to the poor;
His righteousness endures forever;
His horn will be exalted with honor.
 The wicked will see it and be grieved;
 He will gnash his teeth and melt away;
The desire of the wicked shall perish.
   Psalm 112, NKJV

7

The Alaskan summer is a season to behold. The sun rises high in the sky and makes increasingly long arcs from east to west until it nearly circles the horizon. Dusk and dawn blend together and birth a luminescent glow leaving the arctic land in splendid clarity.

The final week of school nears completion. Erik continued his routine of appeasement and lip-service. At the turn of the final hour of the final day of class, Erik and all those like him became free.

"How was your final day, son?" Bill asked him as he walked through the wedged-open door. "You must be feeling some relief."

"In one way or another. I'm just glad to be done with that nonsense for a while," Erik replied, shaking his head.

"Nonsense? I know some of those teachers of yours are nuttier 'an a fruit cake but there's gotta be something you get out of it, don't ya?"

"Not really. I mean, unless worshiping the alter of Upside-Down World is considered valuable. I'm just excited to start going out on the trail with you and Joe and the other guys and start putting some of these rigs to good use!"

"I'm glad you mentioned it. I think it's time you step up the gauge a little bit." Bill pulled a large metal rectangle from under the counter and placed it on top. He used both hands to maneuver the nearly foot-wide device. "You know exactly what this is, don't ya?"

"Why, yes sir. That is a #9, I could spot that a mile away! Looks like this one has a different latch than the ones on the shelf," Erik said touching a piece of brushed metal.

"You are getting a good eye. You remember I told you Paul has a forge he plays with between seasons? I asked him if he wouldn't mind putting together a special rig for you. Those 9's on the shelf work just fine for your average Joe, but the old farts have learned you change the latch here and it won't freeze up near as bad in the frost. More than one wolf has stepped right dead-center on a man's trap and it didn't snap because it was froze open. Joe figured out this new latch and hasn't had a problem yet so long as he doesn't do anything stupid like set it in a river bank," Bill explained. He continued, "and Paul and I made a deal. You pay the regular discount price for the unit as you have been and the metal work can be paid off to Paul when you visit him this summer. He said he has some yard work you could help him with but it shouldn't take too long to settle up. He's no two-bit whore but he ain't the Queen of England, neither."

Erik fondled the tool for some time. "When can we go out, Bill?"

"Soon, Erik," the old man chuckled. "I know the sun has you eager but the river is still pretty high. The waters need to settle a bit 'fore we can go out to where I want to take you."

He watched Erik continue to play with the gift a while longer. "Alright, now. Put that away and get to grading those fox. There'll be plenty of time for foolin' around later."

Erik finished his tasks gleefully and was an all around joy for each of the customers and the tourists who entered the store through the day.

The walk between the bus stop and his house was not far. Erik made the trip in a few minutes, carrying his prize close at his side. With few concerns, he jumped the flimsy steps onto the porch and stepped inside the trailer home. The door was propped open.

"What do you have there?" Bethany asked sweetly.

"Bill at the shop gave it to me. It is a special trap for wolves. His friend makes them custom on his forge and he made this one for me. I am going to go out later this month with them and learn how to set it up," Erik explained happily.

"I see. It looks expensive," Bethany noted.

"It kind of is. Bill made me a really good deal on it like the others." Erik didn't finish his next sentence.

"The others? You have more of those things?" She asked, inquisitive.

"Oh, well, uhh... I mean, I have a few small things but nothing very big or expensive. This is my first real trap." Erik felt sick.

"I see. And, do you think it is right for you to be spending all your money on these..." Her eyes went between Erik, the #9, and back, "things? I mean, we have a lot of bills adding up now that Ed isn't working."

Erik scoffed and shifted his weight. "Mom, Ed got in a bar fight and tried to kill a guy. That shouldn't be my problem," he said with attitude.

"Well, I see it differently so we'll just have to agree to disagree," she said dismissively.

Erik looked at her seriously. "I agree to nothing."

He went into his room and set the #9 on top of the shelf above his closet door. He stood on his chair and assured both conibears and the smaller #2 leg trap were present. He slid them all away from the ledge and out of direct sight. His nausea grew worse.

~

Forgetting his concerns from the previous evening, Erik enjoyed a typically peaceful day at Great North Trapping, Co. with its perpetual aroma of fine tobacco and wood smoke.

After collecting his paycheck for the week, Erik left Bill to lock the doors and chose to walk home enjoying the summer sun. He arrived to his mother's trailer, walked passed his mother nose-deep in her phone, and sat on his bed. Erik set his pack on the desk and looked around the room. *That's queer. I always push my chair back in...* He looked around the room again and noticed his closet door open and a jacket laying on the floor. His stomach sank.

Erik pulled the cheap, folding chair in front of his closet and stood on it. Slowly he raised on his toes and looked across the empty shelf.

No, no, no! Erik could feel sweat beading up and his heart pounded in his ears. He jumped from the chair knocking it against the wall. "Mom! Mom! Where the hell are my traps?!" He yelled as he ran the short distance down the hall. He slid on the worn linoleum.

The woman continued to fondle her phone and paid no attention to the young man.

"Mom!" He shouted. "Damnit! Where are my traps! Where did you take them?" He shouted.

Her eyes didn't leave the screen. "I told you before. We have responsibilities in this house. You said you wanted a job to help pull your own weight around here. I'm just helping you learn how to take responsibility for your actions."

"What?" Erik's voice squeaked. "I have given you half my paycheck for five months!" His voice was almost inaudible. His face was bright red. His eyes started to burn. "Five months! I haven't been holding out on you. I said I would help with money and I have! I bought those with my money, my half. You stole them from me. They were mine. Where did you take them?"

"I sold them and paid the bills. It wasn't much, anyway."

"They weren't worth much but they were mine! They were special." The young man struggled to keep a wall of emotion behind him.

The woman dropped her hands and flopped her phone in her lap. "You know, Erik. You should be grateful. If I didn't know you had such a passion for torturing animals you might have become some crazy lunatic ending up on daytime TV. Now, why can't you just be a normal boy and spend your money on something useful." She said seriously.

"Torturing animals? Something useful? I don't even know what that means? You stole my property! Those meant something to me." His voice started to shake.

"Yeah, something useful. I don't know, maybe buy us some new movies or something? Just stop playing around with all that hokey shit and get a real job."

Unable to find another word, Erik scoffed once in disbelief and walked out. First he walked down the sidewalk, then jogged, then ran as hard as he could down the main street out of the low-rent residential neighborhood. He pushed hot air through his burning lungs until he felt faint, then pushed harder. Through the commercial district he ran until he came to a familiar strip of kitschy gift shops and family-owned business squeezed by nameless, faceless chain stores. He cut hard and ran into the door of his work with both hands. He crashed into the locked door and nearly hit his head. He held himself up by the door handle until his legs gave out below him. He slid to the ground with his back against the door.

"Erik? What in God's name are you doing here?" A familiar voice asked from above. Bill noted the young man's face when their eyes met. "Erik! What is wrong?"

Bill worked to his knees and sat on the sidewalk beside the broken young man and put his arm around him and held his shoulder. Erik buried his face between his arms but could contain his agony no longer. He tried to speak but could make no sound between his muffled wails.

"Come now, it'll be alright. Whatever it is it'll be alright."

After some time, Bill pulled himself up and pulled his keys from his pocket. He unlocked the door and helped Erik stand. They went inside and sat in the fine leather chairs set out for guests near the counter.

"Okay, now please tell me, what is this all about? You are about torn in two," Bill asked.

Erik took another deep breath and wiped his nose again with his sleeve.

"My mom stole the traps and sold them. All of them." He wiped his nose and eyes, again. "The conibears, the 2, the 9, all of them. She sold them all!" Erik contained the next wave of emotion.

"I am so sorry, Erik. Damnit all! I am so sorry. Damn." Bill rested both hands on his knees and shook his head. "It's alright, Erik. It wasn't much money, after all. A few hundred dollars. We'll replace your equipment. This isn't anything that can't be fixed."

Erik started to calm down. His eyes were burning red and his nose still ran but he looked up to Bill. "You're right. I know. It's just, that's not the point. She is always like that!" Erik shook his head and thought about what he said. "No. She isn't always like that. That's the worse part. She teases me with these periods of being nice, making me think she isn't all bad. Then she turns on a dime and hits me when I don't expect it! One day she is just fine and normal and the next day she steals my stuff and says I am sick for wanting to torture animals! If she was just the same every fucking day maybe I could handle it better!" The tears came back.

"I just..." He continued. "I just don't know how much longer I can take it."

"Now listen, Erik. You aren't planning on doing something real stupid, are you?" Bill asked, stern and clear.

"Stupid, like kill myself?" Erik asked.

"I was thinking along those lines."

Erik thought for several moments. "No. I would not do that. I would run, far far away. I would disappear. I would find a new life, but I wouldn't end it."

"Okay. A runaway I can handle. I couldn't handle the other. Not anymore. You are too special in this world to lose over such a stupid thing."

Both men sat for many more moments.

"Erik, I don't know a whole lot about what is going on at home but I have gathered enough that I have some advice. You can take it or leave it and I won't hold it against you if you say I'm outta line." Bill paused and breathed deeply. "There comes a time in every man's life that he has to make a decision. Now, the good God above seldom gives us the choice of when that decision has to be made. Some men have the luxury of waiting all their lives to prepare but others, well... some men get dealt a bad hand in life and it sounds like you got a real bad draw. It ain't fair but that's not the name of the game. Again, I might be speaking out of turn here but it sounds to me like maybe you will have a decision to make sooner than later. It isn't about the traps. They are just pieces of metal. The point is about a man's spirit. I know we are supposed to be stoic creatures of granite, and sometimes we are. We need to be strong for our wives and our children and the whole community. But a man still has a heart and it can be broke just like a lady's. A lady will let you know when you're hurting her but a man just takes it. He keeps taking it until he can't take it no more and he just wakes up different. You can't tell when it's gunna break but you know its gunna. Erik, I am here to tell you your heart is gunna break and once it does, even God Almighty can't piece it back together. Now, I've walked this line myself a time or two and come damn close to walking right off the ledge. You don't want that but you are on your way." He paused to let his words soak in a moment longer. "I suggest you start thinking about an escape plan. Don't do anything rash and don't do anything while you are worked up. But it might be wise of you to start thinking about what your future might look like."

Erik calmly listened to the old man. He sat still with his hands folded in his lap. "Yeah. I have been thinking about that. It just sounds weird to hear someone else say it. All of it. Everything you said was true. It isn't about the traps. And I do feel like my heart is breaking. Maybe it's too late..." Erik choked again and looked away.

"No. Now listen to me, Erik. You ain't broke. Not yet. You are too sensitive a young man and care too much to have a broken heart. I won't allow such nonsense!" Bill shook his finger.

"Okay," he replied quietly.

"Why don't you go home for the night. Keep your head down and let it run off your back. Get a good night sleep, at least best you can manage. Get some rest, come in tomorrow and we'll see about your stolen gear. Don't worry about that. We'll figure something out. For tonight, keep yourself in order and come in tomorrow. Do we have a plan?"

"Yes. Thank you, Bill... It's just, so... stupid. All of it."

"You are half right. It is stupid but it's also evil. No one should have to go through such trials like that but some men have to. The strongest men are forged from the hottest fires and you are going to be a helluva man."

Erik helped Bill stand and walked together to the door.

"Now, before I found you I was coming back to the shop for somethin' but I can't remember for the life of me what it was." Bill looked around and squinted through his glasses. "Whatever it was, it'll be here in the morning," he said lackadaisically.

~

The morning was warm from the midnight sun. Erik left home early and walked through the park taking the scenic route to work. Chickadees chirped, chipmunks worried. Life went on with little interruption.

Erik picked up his pace and reached the door one minute before the store officially opened. The store unofficially opened an hour early when Bill and his friends enjoyed coffee and smoked a pipe or cigar. They sat in the classy leather chairs Erik had sat in so heavy the day before.

"Erik, good morning!" Came from the group. He recognized Joe as a regular but didn't know the third man.

"Come here, son. Sit on the counter. We've been discussing your problem and might have a solution. Now, this isn't a plan. Until you are 18 you are property of your mother and father, at least that's what the judge says. So if you run away the law will go after you and we can't help. All roads lead to this shop and everyone here, so we can't get involved. You following me?" Bill asked. The other men were equally serious.

"Yessir, I understand. No matter what I decide I won't get anyone else involved but me and I am not going to hurt anyone."

"Good. Now, if we were to give you a plan and the law found out, that would count as helping you and we'd all be complicit in a crime and none of us here have a ticker that'll last one night in jail on a concrete bench. Every man has been in the slammer a time or two or he ain't livin', but one of the pleasures of getting old is having a comfortable bed to lay in..."

The unfamiliar man interrupted, "I don't lay for twelve minutes before I have to get up an' pee. What are you talking about pleasures of getting old?"

"Amen," Joe laughed.

"So as I was sayin'," Bill continued, "we can't help you or even give you a plan. But, what I thought we might do is have a conversation among ourselves and you can just sit over there and listen. After all, it's after 8am and you are on the clock. The time card says so. So, you just go ahead and get to work shufflin' some papers on the counter if you read me." Erik gave a subtle nod to the group.

"So boys, you were tellin' me about your friend out there past Paxson," Bill asked the two men.

"Yeah. I am not sure if you've met him before. Andy is his name. I can't think of his last name at the moment. We used to run a line together back when I lived in Tok. We had a line snaking all the way through the range," the man started to smile at this memories. "Yeah, boys. We had 83 miles of good line and ran it end-to-end in a circuit. It was good times, but the Parks got onto us and we never did finish that last year. Just got too risky..."

Bill redirected, "no, I have not met this Andy. Say I might want to meet the man, how might I come across such a character?"

The man remembered his cue, "oh right. Well, the easiest way I'd figure to find him if I didn't know where to look would be to find your way past Summit Lake to Black Rapids and start working west along the range. There are only a handful of fellers back there and he keeps as close a' eye on the trails as anyone else."

"Well, you know, my car has been kind of on the fritz lately. What do you recommend I do?" Bill asked.

Joe jumped in. "I'd first tell the old lady to get out and relax the springs 'n maybe the tires would roll."

Joe and the unfamiliar man both chuckled. Bill looked at them cross and said, "oh, bite me."

"No, no thank you," Joe replied. Erik held his laughter.

"So, as I was saying about my car problems... Do you have any suggestions, Herb?"

"Well, why don't you just hitch? There's plenty of good folk out there on the road that'll pick up a traveler and so long as the guy don't look too strung out or have a pile of propane tanks in the back I'd probably ride along."

"Don't think I need to worry about Troopers?" Bill asked.

"Well, I guess it's always something to think about but so long as this is still Alaska it shouldn't be a big concern. Especially if they aren't looking for you," Herb answered.

"That's a relief. But you know, I am still a little worried about how I might eat out there on the trail looking for Andy, and who's to say Andy will even want to visit with me?" Bill inquired.

"Right. If I was traveling afoot on the trails, I wouldn't be caught dead without my kit to set some snares. Best if I had a gun but I could get by if I was in a real pinch, a real survival kind of situation, you know? A man doesn't need much if he has the will to make it happen." The men nodded and Herb continued, "Andy can be a mite tough to get used to. He comes on strong but he has a soft heart. If I was in real trouble, he's the guy I'd want to see. He doesn't make himself real easy to like but I can't think of no one else I could rely on better. He is a goddamn saint is what he is. No one has ever done more for a man in need than Andy." Herb thought for a moment. "Well, he don't bite, anyway."

"So get on that side of the range and just start wandering the trails. That's it?" Bill asked genuinely confused.

"That's about right." Herb nodded.

"Well, thanks for the talk, ladies. Maybe I'll make it for happy hour tonight if I can hitch up my wife to the truck in time." Bill said sarcastically looking at Joe.

Erik made close mental note of the conversation to keep in his back pocket.

~

"Thanks for the cash, Bill," Erik said as he signed a pay stub.

"Oh, don't thank me. You more than earn it around here. Joe is pert' near ready to sell off his youngest daughter just so he can buy a new string from you. You have a gift of connectin' with people, Erik," Bill replied counting out three one-hundred dollar bills and one fifty. "Protect that gift like it's somethin' real special."

"I will," he replied. Erik picked up his wages and tucked them into his billfold. "Oh, and remember I won't be in next week. I am leaving Monday for my dad's place."

"That's right. Thanks for reminding me. You gunna be gone the whole week, right?" Bill asked with a frown.

"Yep. That's what the judge tells me, anyway. The old man gets a week every other Christmas and the week before school."

"What a bad deal, for the whole bunch of ya." Bill shook his head. "At least the lawyers' kids are doing good."

"I can hardly blame the guy for cutting bait. I will probably do the same thing when the right opportunity comes along! Just another year and a half.

Well, I guess closer to two..." Erik's smile faded at the thought.

"Just remember like I says: you don't know what offer God will put on the table but you'll know the right decision when you see it. It won't take much thinkin' at all when the time comes. You'll know it. God just talks to some men like that and he's got you on speed dial, I'm sure of it."

Erik tapped the counter with his hand and said plainly, "I'll see you next week, Bill. Oh, and try to keep this place half-way put together, please? I finally got it in order."

Bill laughed. "Don't you worry. Everything will be right where you left it."

The young man picked up his pack and headed for the door. He turned to give a quick wave as he left

~

No one was home when Erik unlocked the door. "Guess the witch is out trying a new broomstick," he uttered as he looked around the living room.

Erik kicked off his shoes and walked to his room. He tilted his head and looked across the vertical titles of books on his small case attached to the end of his desk. He pulled out a well-worn book and sat on the edge of his bed. He ran his fingers across the leather cover and felt the cracks forming along the spine. He set it to his side and pulled his billfold out from his pocket. He took two hundred dollar bills from the small wad and felt the heavy paper. Erik opened the book halfway and laid the two bills tight to the spine and closed it. *Wait... huh?* He opened the book again and flipped through a few pages. Nothing but text. He flipped a few more, more quickly. Nothing. His heart instantly raced as he thumbed through the rest of the pages, tearing a few as he turned several at a time. Erik slowed, then stopped. He knew. "Un-fucking-believable," he said calmly.

He sat on the edge of his bed for a few more moments considering his next move. He picked the book up again from his lap and turned to the single obstacle making a break in the pages. He picked out the two bills and placed them on his wallet next to him. He looked back to the open page.

Så hendte det en dag at Guds sønner kom og stilte sig frem for Herren, og blandt dem kom også Satan og stilte sig frem for Herren. Og Herren sa til Satan: Hvor kommer du fra? Satan svarte Herren: Jeg har faret og flakket omkring på jorden. Da sa Herren til Satan: Har du gitt akt på min tjener Job? For det er ingen på

jorden som han(-)en ulastelig og rettskaffen mann, som frykter Gud og viker fra det onde; ennu er han like ulastelig, og du har uten grunn egget mig til å ødelegge ham.
Job 2:1-3

Again there was a day when the sons of God came to present themselves before the Lord, and Satan came also among them to present himself before the Lord. And the Lord said to Satan, "From where do you come?" Satan answered the Lord and said, "From going to and fro on the earth, and from walking back and forth on it." Then the Lord said to Satan, "Have you considered My servant Job, that there is none like him on the earth, a blameless and upright man, one who fears God and shuns evil? And still he holds fast to his integrity, although you incited Me against him, to destroy him without cause."
Job 2:1-3

Erik again closed the book. His decision had been made.

8

Dawn came to southcentral Alaska just as the lingering night sun rose over the crest of the Chugach mountains. Erik woke from a nap feeling cramped and uncomfortable but at peace. He listened to the creek for several minutes before moving. It sounded alive, water moving freely between the rocks. It washed sand from the banks and carved new channels across the bars. All the creatures from all over came to the creek and drank from it and found new inspiration replenishing their weary spirits. He watched and he listened and he thought, and he felt.

Erik worked his way out of the dirt dugout beside the creek and sat on the bank. He sat and stretched his feet and flexed his toes. He rubbed feeling back into his calves and legs. Then he sat a while longer. He pulled his backpack up next to him and pulled the rainfly off and tucked it back in its pouch. He removed his wool sweater and put it away, also. It was going to warm up quickly. Erik stood, swung his small pack onto his back and slid his arms through the straps in one motion. He made one big step across the creek channel and scrambled his way up the hillside. Once through the shrubs and willows, he stepped onto the well-maintained gravel walking path. In a few minutes he was beyond the park, on the road, and walking north.

~

"So, you a hiker or somethin'?" A man in his early-30's asked. His red checkered shirt matched his faded red pickup.

"Yeah, I guess," Erik replied, nonchalant. He sat in the passenger seat with his backpack between his legs, his hands in his lap.

"Well, you are or you aren't, aren't you? I mean, it'd be kind of silly to just decide one day to go hitching along then climb Denali the next without some kind of plan, don't you think?" The man's eyes focused between the road and Erik's face. He kept one hand on the steering wheel, the other fixed on the gearshift.

"I just don't think 'hiker' is the right word is all. 'Explorer'? 'Adventurer' maybe? 'Wanderer'. Yeah, that's the right word. I guess I'm a wanderer."

"Is that like being a runaway without a destination?"

"Oh, I have a destination," Erik answered quickly.

"And where exactly is that destination?"

"Anywhere else." Erik kept looking out the window and beyond the horizon.

The man looked at Erik for a long moment until the rumble strips reminded him of the road. He allowed the silence to linger before speaking again.

"I don't mean to get nosy but what are you running away from, anyway?" He asked.

"I need to spend my time doing other things than what I've been doing," Erik replied.

"Don't I at least get a hint? I mean, if you knocked over some bank I need to know if I should expect lights in my mirror." The man seemed only half joking.

Erik chuckled at the amusing thought. "No, I didn't rob a bank. I just need to get away from that place. There was nothing good to come from staying there."

"You have a bad fight with your folks or your dad beat you or something? You have some battle scars on your face, I could see that before I picked you up."

"My whole life has been one bad fight. Yesterday was nothing new... but that doesn't mean today can't be different if I want it bad enough." Erik looked at the man and back out the windshield.

"You know, relationships are tough. Sometimes you just have to stick it out," the driver said

Erik was silent. He took a deep breath, closed his eyes, released, then looked at the driver. "No. You don't 'just have to stick it out'. That is a setup by shitty people that are tough to get along with. Relationships are not tough. There are tough people that try to convince you the problems are in the relationship and not in themselves because if the problem is them, they have nowhere to look but inward and nobody to blame but themselves. If they convince you that it is the relationship that is the problem, they have also convinced you that the problem is at least half yours. They lead you into self-doubt and convince you it is you who is difficult and it is you who is the problem and it is you who needs to change.

"And, I say, if there was some proclivity I had to become involved with such a sophist and manipulator and I didn't run the other way at the first sign in the first hour the first time we met, then they are probably right. Then I do have a problem and I do need to confront those.

"And when a shitty person says to me 'relationships are tough and if you don't stay with me then you are running away from all your problems', I say 'no, you are a shitty person and I will not tolerate such abuse in my life.'" Erik shifted and looked out the side window.

Silence lingered for many more moments. "Hey, listen man. I didn't mean to offend you or anything. I was just trying to help," he said half-hearted.

"I appreciate you trying to make small talk but you aren't helping when you say things like that. One-liners and truisms don't help and telling someone to stay in an abusive relationship is even worse, yet." Erik was still looking out the side window.

"I wasn't telling you to stay in an abusive relationship," he replied indignantly. "I just don't think kids ought to be running away is all."

"That's exactly what your words mean, Steven," Erik turned and faced him again. "That is exactly what you are saying when you tell me that 'relationships are tough' and that I just need to 'stick it out'. Pay attention to what you are saying. Think about what those words mean! I'm not trying to be a dick about it but it is so important that words match their meaning. So many people just make mouth noises without knowing what they are saying, it's... it's one of the worst sins there is."

Steven drove the truck without saying another word until they approached a T marking the end of that highway. "So, Erik, I need to know if you are going north or south. I am turning for Valdez here. I am happy to bring you along but if you are northbound then I'll have to drop you in Glennallen."

"I am going north," Erik replied.

"Okay. Will you let me buy you lunch first before we part ways? I want to thank you for being so straight with me. Not many guys out there will tell it like it is to a complete stranger. I think I owe it to you. There's a roadhouse just before town with pretty good soup. Esther makes it from scratch. Will you join me for lunch?"

"Thank you. Soup sounds great right now," Erik answered.

The hum of off-road tires settled down as Steven pulled his tired pickup into the gravel lot. He parked on the side of the building next to a similar model truck with wooden stake-sides. Two vans and a motor home were parked in front. All three had license plates from other states.

~

"Be careful Tyler!" The young mother called to her toddler.

"Come on, Leah. Let the kid play around," the child's father said to her.

"I'm just worried he'll break something is all," she said with concern.

"I know you're worried. You're always worried about something. He is having fun and it doesn't look like anyone is bothered by him."

"Oh, maybe you're right. I just don't like that he's around all those..."

A crash and clatter came from behind the young mother. She turned in her chair to find her son on the floor near the corner of the restaurant. A hand-carved sign hung from the ceiling read **GIFTS**. Next to the boy, now sitting on his bottom and crying, were the remnants of a broken coffee mug. The young mother panicked at the sight and quickly jumped from her chair. Before she was completely upright a hand on her shoulder resisted her motion.

"Sit down Leah. I'll take care of this," the father said. His youthful voice reassured her. She stopped, watched him walk to their child, and she sat back down to watch.

"Tyler, from the way you're acting I'm not sure which is more broken, the mug or you!" The father said standing over the scene. He first knelt to get closer to his son, then sat on the floor beside him after brushing away a few ceramic splinters.

"Well, son. It looks like you did a good job on that mug." The boy was still crying and red in his face. His father put his arm around him and pulled the boy close to his chest. "Come on, now. It's alright. We'll get this sorted out, you just get yourself calmed down."

"I... I... didn't mean to!" The child cried between his sobs.

"I am sure you didn't intend to break the mug but when you are running around in a gift shop looking at things, it's a risk that you'll drop something or knock it over and it will break. It isn't the end of the world but it is something you need to think about before running around in a store."

The boy looked at the shattered mug and started to settle, somewhat.

"The first thing is I'm glad you're okay. Looks like you just slipped and fell on your butt?" The father asked.

"Mmmhm," the boy sounded.

"Okay. Now that we know you're safe, the next thing we need to do is figure out what to do about this mug. There are other people that might want to come look at gifts so we need to get it cleaned up. We also need to pay the lady for the damaged mug since she can't sell it anymore," he explained. He held his young son into his chest until the sobs nearly abated.

"How do I do that?" The child asked through his running nose.

The waitress was standing to the side watching the whole scene. She said, "you don't have to worry about it, sir. It's alright. He didn't mean any harm." Her voice was deep for a woman but still pleasantly feminine.

The young father looked to the woman and replied, "thanks ma'am but it's important to me that my son cleans up the mess and pays for the mug." He was not rude but he was firm in his statement.

"Well, I'll at least bring the broom over for him." She opened a small closet next to the kitchen walkway and brought out a broom and dust pan. When she returned, the boy was standing and received the broom without fuss and struggled to leverage the long handle.

"There you go, Tyler. You're doing great. Here, I'll hold the dust pan and you sweep the pieces in." After a minute of ineffectively swinging the broom twice his height, his father picked up a few of the big pieces and set them in the dust pan. He stood and said to his son, "you're doing pretty good. Now let's trade and I'll sweep the last of it and you can hold the pan for me. Deal?"

Without replying, the boy handed his father the broom and made the switch. The young father quickly swept the remaining pieces and splinters and some dust into a pile and showed his son how to hold the pan. Once the pile of debris was in the pan, the father picked it up and dumped it in the trash can the waitress placed by them. She pulled it back next to the entrance once he was finished.

The boy and his father gave their tools back to the lady. The father then squatted to his hams and sat eye-level with his son. "That was a good job, Tyler. I am proud of you doing so well getting that cleaned up. Now we have to pay for the damages. It is important that we make it right with the restaurant owner. The sign says that mugs cost five dollars. Do you have five dollars in your pocket?"

The boy pulled his jeans pockets inside-out and came up with two quarters and a dime.

"How much money is that?" The father inquired.

The boy struggled with the arithmetic and answered with a look of uncertainty.

"These are quarters and they are twentyfive cents each. The dime is ten cents. So that is twenty five, fifty, sixty cents," he counted as he pointed to the coins in his son's hand. "It looks like you don't have five dollars. We can ask the waitress if they will accept what you have or you can borrow money from me and you can pay me back. What would you like to do?"

"I don't know," he said as he tried to understand what he was asked.

"I suggest you borrow five dollars from me this time and pay me back by doing work around the house. But if we do that, I need you to promise me that you will pay me back out of your allowance or by doing extra work."

"Okay," the boy said.

"Do you promise to pay me back if I loan you the money to pay for the mug?"

"Yeah, I promise," the boy said looking at his father's face.

"Okay," the man pulled out a five dollar bill from his wallet and gave it to his son. "There is five dollars to pay for the mug. Don't forget to tell the lady you are sorry for the trouble."

The boy took the bill and stretched his arm to the waitress standing a few feet away. "I'm sorry for breaking your cup," he said.

"Oh thank you. You are such a responsible young man." The lady took the bill and smiled in admiration as the father and son walked back to the table.

"How did I do?" He asked his wife as he helped his son into the booster seat.

"Robby..." She was flushed and emotional.

He looked at his wife and smiled. She was more beautiful today at this roadside eatery than she had ever been to him before.

~

"Geeze, by the way that lady is about to burst into tears you'd swear the guy just proposed," Steven said to Erik as they sat at their table.

Erik looked across the room as he sat in his chair. "Yeah, sure looks like they're in the middle of something real special."

The waitress greeted the men and gave them both a menu.

"Thanks, Esther. What's for soup today?" Steven asked.

"Today is crab chowder and buffalo chili's on everyday. Both are made from scratch, as always," she said giving Steven a wink. "Who's your friend?"

"This here is Erik. He is a wanderer and a philosopher. I figured I owed him lunch after we've been talking for so long."

"Well ain't that somethin'. You just ridin' 'round the state Erik?" She asked.

"Yes, ma'am. I suppose you could say that. Truth is I just need to spend some time in the wilderness and figure out who I am."

She smiled at Erik again and turned to Steven. "You listen to this kid, Steven, and you might learn something."

Steven laughed and said, "you have no idea how true that is, Esther."

"Alright now, you fellas know what you want?"

"Erik, I am buying but I don't want you to hold back. The chowder they make with real king crab and it is thick, not like that watery crap from a can. I'm having the chili but you can order whatever you want."

"Uhh, I guess I'll have the chowder!" He said.

"You gentlemen want some iced tea while we get you fixed up?" She asked.

"That sounds lovely," Erik said. Steven nodded in affirmation as he handed his menu back to her.

~

Erik walked four miles before anyone stopped. Motorhomes and trucks with campers and vans and buses of all sizes passed by in a stead flow. Sometimes the passengers looked at the traveler walking on the shoulder as they passed by. Sometimes they only looked forward.

An old couple in a camper van pulled off into the dirt ahead of Erik and waited for him to catch up. The old woman in the driver's seat rolled her window down and her husband talked across her.

"Where you headed?" His voice was gravely.

"Hi, sir. Ma'am. I'm just trying to make my way to Black Rapids about an hour's drive north of here."

"I know where it's at. What's for you there?" He asked. His wife's head turned to watch each speaker.

"I, uhh, plan to meet a friend there," Erik replied. He didn't feel confident in his response.

The old man looked at Erik's backpack, obviously prepared for a light trip outdoors. "You plannin' on doin' some hikin'? Doesn't look like you have much of a loadout."

"Oh, I have everything I'll need to get by, I suspect. A man doesn't need much if he has the will to make it happen." Erik was more confident with that response.

"Well, Joann. I think the Lord would be mighty cross with us if we were to get in the way of this gentleman and his mission. I'm sure we could give him a lift a few miles down the way, save 'em some trouble?" His wife nodded and smiled.

He turned his seat sideways and opened the sliding van door. "Just set you kit there. That's fine. You can take a seat on the bench by the galley. There's no belt but we'll ask Joann to keep this tank under a hundred and we'll be just fine."

"Thank you, sir. I sure appreciate the ride. It was getting pretty hot along that pavement," Erik said. He pulled a water bottle out of his bag and drank from it, wiping his forehead with a handkerchief.

"Are you hungry? When's the last time you ate?" The man asked before buckling his lap belt.

"I had lunch a few hours ago."

"Okay, that was half of what I asked. Here," the man stood from his seat again and stepped to a small cabinet. The camper van was just tall enough for the man to stand with his head ducked. He dug out a sandwich bag and handed it to Erik. "That's some salmon we smoked last week. It's a little on the salty side but not too bad for my first try."

Erik opened the bag, took out a piece, and handed it back.

"Oh, no. You can keep it. There is plenty more where that came from."

Erik looked at the man for a moment and acknowledged with a smile. He slipped the baggie into the top pouch of his bag next to him. "Well, thank you for the snack."

"It's no problem at all. Now, where are you comin' from? Oh, and I don't think I caught your name earlier. I'm Cal and that there is Joann."

"I'm glad to meet you Cal, Joann. My name is Erik. My mom lives in

Anchorage and my dad lives on Kodiak."

"I see. Well, please forgive me for being so frank but you ain't but a pup. What's a youngster like you doing hitchin' in the middle of nowhere?" Cal asked.

"I guess I'm just looking for something."

"And you expect that something to be all the way out here?"

Erik pondered for a moment before answering carefully. "I wouldn't expect to find it anyplace else."

A new voice came from the cab. "Lot's of folks go out looking for something, but you, my friend, you have something to find," Joann said with an old lady warble.

Erik looked at her in the rear-view mirror, then back to Cal. "Until I start, I'll never know."

~

Erik waved at the camper van as it pulled onto the road and honked. He turned to face an unblazed trail. The well-beaten path was now at his back.

B

Hast thou not known?
hast thou not heard,
that the everlasting God, the Lord,
the Creator of the ends of the earth,
fainteth not, neither is weary?
there is no searching of his understanding.

He giveth power to the faint;
and to them that have no might
he increaseth strength.
Even the youths shall faint and be weary,
and the young men shall utterly fall:
But they that wait upon the Lord shall renew their strength;
they shall mount up with wings as eagles;
they shall run, and not be weary;
and they shall walk, and not faint.
Isaiah 40:28-31 KJV

9

Where is hope for the forlorn?
Where is courage for the despondent?
Where is knowledge for the ignorant?
Where is love for the hated?
Where is rage for the wicked?
Where is mercy for the tormented?
Where is adventure for the wandering?
Where is shame for the deserving?
Where is peace for the haunted.
Where is justice?

Erik worked along a slope of scree and rock following no determined route. Farther across the hillside and a little higher was his destination, a large boulder with a slight projection. He climbed to the top with some effort and sat on the warm surface. The late afternoon sun was still high.

"Alright, guess it's time to see if I'm lost," he said to himself. He opened his pack and drank the remainder of one water bottle. He carried two. Erik pulled out a folded map of maintained mushing trails, one of a few items he gave to customers at the store for free.

There's the highway running along the valley. The Delta, alright. And here I am on this face. Looks like... "Two miles that way," he pointed to the direction, "and I'll be on the main system. God, I sure hope this is what they meant."

Erik climbed off the natural lookout and dropped the last foot onto uneven ground. He commenced his trek along the easiest route across the face and back below the treeline. A little more than one hour had passed since he stood on the rock to when he crossed an overgrown break in the forest. "Well, I guess this is it. Sure doesn't look well-traveled to me."

He stayed on the trail and hiked west farther into the trees. By his watch it was nearly night. The sun now dipped below the skyline for the first time in weeks. Dusk would throw a dull light across the land if the dense clouds rolling in hadn't covered the sky.

Erik sat against a birch tree and fished out the bag of smoked salmon the kind couple had given him. He ate the last three pieces and tucked the bag away. Erik put on his wool sweater and rain jacket, unfolded a light blanket and laid down to sleep.

02:12am

It was just light enough to see his hand in front of his face and a blurred outline of trees. Nothing more. In only a few days the nights went from warm and active to cold and slow. Seasons transitioned quickly in the north and those who did not prepare would soon fear the consequences.

Erik curled tighter under his blanket and floated between discomfort and dream for several more hours.

~

"Okay, Erik. It's that time. Time to get up and get moving," he said to himself. With a great stretch, his back popped and his feet poked out from under the blanket. He brushed his teeth with a sparing amount of water, put away his bedroll, and continued walking the trail.

Before he traveled much distance that morning, Erik hopped over a small creek crossing the path. He found a spot with few willows and knelt to the water. He splashed and scrubbed his face and hair. The cold water was refreshing. He pulled out both of his water bottles and filled them full. He drank one halfway down before holding his head from brain freeze. He refilled the bottle full and secured both to the sides of his pack.

By noontime Erik's hunger caught up with him. For several hours he walked through a green tunnel of willow, birch, and other vegetation of the boreal forest.

"Dang. This is tough stuff to travel through," he said as he kicked over some grass to sit on. Below the grass was moss. Dampness wicked up Erik's jeans.

"Okay, so according to this map there is an old cabin just another half-mile farther... or, at least it's a half-mile from where I think I am." Erik looked up to try making out a distinct peak on the ridgeline through the trees. He ate a few pieces of jerky before continuing his course. A chill lingered in the air under thick cloud cover.

"Is that it?" He asked himself. "That ain't nothing but a rotten old shed."

Erik walked around the fallen-down structure. It was ten feet off the trail but almost invisible, nearly vanished, absorbed back into the earth.

"Yeah, look at that. That's it for sure. Looks like the skunks moved in a long time ago." He looked around and kicked a rusty can into a pile of others. "Jesus. I hope this isn't where that Andy guy lived. I'm going to be SOL if he isn't around here somewhere else."

After a while longer of exploring the area around the old camp, Erik decided to make camp of his own. He walked a ways in the direction of a small creek and fixed a small conibear trap to a spruce tree with sign of some rodent activity. Halfway back to the camp, Erik set a small snare on what looked like a game trail, but he wasn't sure. *Worth a try*, he thought.

Back at camp he pulled what was left of the front door off its remaining hinge and set it against a tree on its side. He grabbed a few more boards and stacked them up against the door from the ground up. He set his pack under the make-do shelter and started collecting firewood. Spruce limbs, broken boards from the dilapidated structure, and other scraps made a good stock of fuel. Erik collected a few strings of birch bark and sat down at the edge of his lean-to. He used a cheap lighter and had a solid fire in little time. He worked his teepee of sticks together and tended the fire. For a good while, Erik sat on the duffy ground against his tree, holding his knees into his chest and watched the embers glow.

As darkness approached late in the evening, Erik stacked a few of the larger pieces of repurposed boards on the bed of coals. He stood and walked down his trail to check the trap and snare before walking-light faded for good. The snare was untouched but the conibear trap had snapped. *Nothing.* He sat next to the spruce and played with the trap a few minutes more before resetting it. *What is that smell?* "Huhh?" He turned and looked toward camp. "Oh, shit!" He exclaimed.

Erik started toward camp in a sprint when a few strides later his foot caught and came out from under him. He fell forward and landed on his left side. A sharp pain jumped from his wrist followed by a warm tingle up his forearm. Erik rolled upright, removed the snare wire caught on his shoe and stumbled up. He ran to the lean-to shelter and kicked the burning door off the tree and over onto the ground. He kicked the large fire apart and scratched dirt and duff onto it, knocking down the flames. He turned around again and kicked and stomped at his backpack now smoldering with a foul, burnt-plastic stench. "Jesus fucking Christ. When will it end?" He swore. He kicked more dirt onto the backpack, and again, more furiously kicking dirt onto the melted scrap. Erik looked at the fire now nearly out, clenched his fists to white knuckles, and released his emotions into the forest. No one called back.

His strength dissipated and he felt lightheaded. He laid on the ground, hugged his knees, and fell asleep.

~

Bill arrived to his store an hour before opening as usual. He took one mitten off and searched his jacket pocket for the keys. He fumbled with the ring and dropped it on the ground. "Dadgummit," he uttered as he bent to pick up the keys.

"If I knew this was what it'd be like gettin' old I might've reconsidered," he strained as he stood back up. He fiddled with the lock and opened the door. As he turned to shut the door behind him he looked down. A sheet of paper on the floor caught his eye. "That's weird. Must've been slid under the door."

He picked up the paper but he didn't need to read it. He already knew what it said.

God called. I answered. EL

He folded the paper and tucked it in his breast pocket. "Best of luck," he whispered. "Best of luck."

~

I am so cold... It was dark when he opened his eyes. A dusting of snow covered the mountain sides, the camp, and crusted over Erik. The involuntary quivering of his arms and legs and chest almost hurt. His muscles ached and his stomach was nauseous.

Erik slowly rolled onto his back, then sat up. His muscles were stiff with chill. His wrist throbbed with each heartbeat. His forearm felt like it was burning from the inside out. He looked at it and noticed dark crusty smears all across his skin. He stood in the greyscale of dawn and found his pack, now damp with snow. With numb fingers he found his handkerchief stuffed in a side pouch. He clumsily wrapped it over the oozing gash and tied it wrong-handed. Next he felt for the sandwich bag with his lighter. He stumbled to a birch tree and excised a large square of bark with his pocket knife. Back to the defunct camp, he scraped the snow crust off the dirt with his shoe and placed the fire materials there. With less patience and more effort, Erik built a new fire after several attempts to light the now-damp wood. The cheap lighter was weak in the cold temperature and his nondominant hand struggled to flick it with sufficient speed. He grew the fire to be of large size and sat next to it. He would not be leaving for some time.

It was mid-morning when the sun crested the high mountain ridge to the south and east. Erik emptied the contents of his pack on the dry side of the burned door laying on the ground. Most of the items were untouched and intact except for his rain jacket which was partly hanging out of the zippered pocket at the time of the incident. Below the rain jacket was his red and white wool sweater, now with a black singe across the reindeer pattern chest. He struggled to put the pullover on, followed by the rain jacket with a large, irregular hole in the lower back. Erik wrapped the untouched blanket around him like a cape and tended the fire until he was warm.

✝

Two are better than one;
because they have a good reward for their labour.
For if they fall, the one will lift up his fellow:
but woe to him that is alone when he falleth;
for he hath not another to help him up.
Ecclesiastes 4:9-10 KJV

10

A man lived alone in the mountains
until he forgot the sound of his own voice.
When he spoke he startled
as though somebody was standing behind him.

"Who's there? Show yourself!" The voice was booming. "I know you're in there. Come out wheres I can see ya!"

Erik panicked and sat still. He was leaning against a tree but the willows were thick around him, concealing him from the intruder.

"You got cotton balls in your ears? If you don't show yourself I'll blast behind every bush 'til I find what's left of ya!" The voice called again.

"O...okay. I'm standing up now." Erik's heart pounded and he felt sick. He tried to stand on shaking legs that barely held his weight.

"Do I need to light a fire under your ass?" He called again.

Erik found his strength and stood up, feeling like he was about to vomit.

"Come on, all the way. Show your face."

As he stood up over the grass and the willows a shotgun came into his view. Behind the barrel was a very large man. He looked well over six feet tall but thin and lanky. His face was well-tanned and weather-worn like old leather. His grey eyes pierced Erik's soul.

"What are you doing here, boy?" He shouted.

"Uhh, I... I'm looking for a guy called Andy. A friend of his sent me here and I have been looking for him," Erik's voice sped up until he was cut-off.

"Someone sent you to find Andy? I know Andy and he doesn't have any friends," he interjected.

"I run away from some bad shit at home and didn't have anywhere else to go and I heard that Andy might be able to help me please sir I'm not lying!" Erik started to panic.

There was a long pause. He then asked, "where's your gun? You have a gun?"

"No, sir! No, I don't have any weapons but a knife," Erik answered quickly.

"What in God's name are you doing in these mountains without a gun!" He exclaimed. "You are damn lucky I found you before the bears did."

He lowered his shotgun and put the sling over his shoulder. "This all your stuff?" He looked at the backpack with sandwich bags on the ground around it.

"Yes, sir. Everything I have is in this bag."

"Pull yourself together and follow me. Shelter is a long ways ahead," the man said as he started walking toward the trail.

~

Erik stumbled over fallen birch and willow thickets and struggled to keep up with the man. The official trail was overgrown but visible, though they did not follow it. The big man carved new paths through the forest. Some routes were obvious to the younger but some were not. Each route they took was different from the last. Across the creek, along the creek. Through the willow, around the willow. No pattern was obvious to Erik as he followed the man but each came together and weaved across the terrain. He also fell behind several times and exerted himself to catch up. After what felt like all afternoon, the man stopped walking. Erik stopped behind him and found what they had stopped for. They arrived at an inconspicuous structure. *I would have walked right past it,* Erik thought to himself.

Once the man saw Erik catch up he opened the door of the abandoned-looking cabin blended with shrubs and vegetation, and stooped his head as he entered. Erik followed inside and was amazed.

"This is a lot bigger than what it looks like on the outside," he said as he looked around the warm interior. The centerpiece of the open room was a large wood stove. The open area was small and cozy feeling. A functional kitchen made one corner with a thin table dividing the spaces. A wood door separated the apparent living area from what looked like a bedroom which was unusual for the typical one-room trapper cabins found in the region.

"Put your bag there," he said pointing at the rug next to the door. "And take off your jacket and sit at the table. I saw you guardin' your arm." He sounded patient.

Erik did as he was told and winced as he pulled his left arm out of the sleeve. He sat on the wood bench and for the first time he could see his injury for what it really was. When he removed the crusted handkerchief he saw a deep puncture where a stick pierced his skin. Black and purple surrounded the wound and redness radiated down his forearm to his wrist which was now swollen to the size of his fist. He could not move it.

The man towered over Erik inspecting his injury. "That's not good, boy. You need to get to the clinic and get that infection stopped before it gets in your blood. Probably need x-rays for that popped wrist, too." He looked out the window from where he was standing. "Too late to leave now but I'll take you out in the morning and you can get on your merry way."

Erik looked at the man in shock. "No! I can't leave. I am here to find Andy. My arm doesn't hurt that bad. I can stand it. No way I'm going back out there!"

"Listen boy, you need to get that infection treated before it spreads. It could kill ya. And if you ever want to wipe your own ass again you'll get that hand straightened out. That's the end of it," the man replied with even less patience than before.

"You didn't hear me. I am not going into town. They will send me back to that hell hole and I ain't going. I'll leave you alone and keep walking if you can tell me where to find Andy but I am not going to town. Shit, I'll leave right now if that's what you want. This is your house. I have no rights here. I don't even know what I'm doing here!"

The man looked at him, then walked into what Erik thought was a bedroom. He came out with a brown bottle and what looked like gauze. "Go wash your arm in the sink and we'll pour some iodine on it. You can stay here tonight but you will leave in the morning." Erik stood up and made two steps to the kitchen area. He looked around the sink but did not find a faucet. Confused, he looked back to the man who was pouring water from a kettle on the stove into a bowl. He handed it to Erik and said, "here, there is a rag under the sink. Use soap."

Erik did as instructed and winced each time he worked the warm rag over the puncture. Brown and dark-red water ran down his arm and off his fingertips with each pass. The water pooled at the bottom of the shallow sink before finding the drain hole and dripping into a bucket below it. Scrubbing the crusted blood was too painful but he did clean off the loose debris from around the wound. "Okay," he said. His stomach was unsettled from the pain. "That's the best I can do."

The man came up behind Erik and looked at his work. "I doubt that's your best," he said sharply. He opened the bottle of brown liquid and poured it across Erik's entire forearm and into the puncture. "Hold still," he said as Erik's arm shook from the awakened nerves.

He capped the bottle and put a gauze square over the site. He tied a piece of cotton cloth around the injured arm, then put his supplies away. "Sit at the table and I will make supper. It will get cold tonight. You can sleep on the floor next to the stove on that bear skin. That will keep ya outta the way."

Erik sat at the table and held his injured wrist with his opposite hand. The red tissue radiated heat. He sat in silence as the man walked between the kitchen and the wood stove which now groaned with heat.

The man dished a soup with what looked like thick chunks of meat. Erik wasn't sure what kind of meat it was and was not sure he should ask. He held the spoon awkwardly and blew on the liquid before sipping it. The man sat across the narrow table and ate his soup quickly. Erik next picked a piece of meat and blew on it. He ate it and was surprised by how flavorful it was. "What kind of meat is this?" he asked.

The man took two more spoonfuls before answering. "Caribou."

"Is that why the broth is so rich? I have heard that caribou fat is really rich but I've never had it before."

The man didn't answer.

"Are you Andy?"

The man didn't answer.

"I really thank you for what you're doing but I am out here to find Andy."

The man looked at Erik. "Why are you looking for Andy?"

"Because, because I have nothing else to look for."

The man waited. He saw desperation in Erik's face. "And you think finding Andy is going to fix that?"

"I don't know. But I've got nothing else left. I've got nowhere else to turn. This is it. This is all I got." Despite his attempt to hold it back, emotions rose to his face.

"What are you running from?" He asked.

"I am not running from anything. I am running toward something. I just don't know what it is, yet." Erik replied.

"What about your family? Aren't your parents going to be looking for you?"

"I have no family in this world. I have relatives but they lost me a long time ago."

The man thought on what he heard. "Time for lights out. Lay over there where I told you and you'll be out of the road."

A few minutes later he disappeared into the bedroom. Erik laid on the bear rug and tucked his blanket around him. He laid on his uninjured side and curled inward toward the stove beside him. He was lulled to rest as waves of warmth reached his heart.

~

Erik rose to consciousness by the sound of a raven flying overhead. Much light came through the kitchen window but he was unsure of the hour. He felt like he had slept for a very long time.

He rose to his feet and said to the empty room, "hello?" He looked past the open door to the bedroom and asked again, "hello?" Erik then went outside and looked around the cabin and found nothing and no one. He went back inside and stood by the stove.

"Might as well make myself useful, I guess."

Erik grabbed a straw broom from the corner of the room where a few other tools were leaning against the wall. He swept the kitchen and the area around the stove with his good hand and used his injured hand to balance the handle. He opened the bedroom door all the way and stepped inside. It was a small room. A pile of hides laid against the wall in what looked like a makeshift bed. Adjacent to it was a simple desk obviously made by hand by the roughness of it. Erik stepped in front of the desk and an old typewriter sat on top catching his eye. It was well use and well worn. Several letters were no longer legible on the metal keys. Next to the typing machine was a picture. Erik picked it up by the wood frame and looked at it. It was quite old and was starting to yellow around the edges. A man and what looked like his wife were holding each other in front of lake. They were looking at the camera and smiling. A young boy was standing in front of them and laughing at something behind the photographer. "They look so happy..." Erik said.

He set the picture back on the desk and finished looking around the room. There were no other pictures or decorations.

He swept the floor under the desk and beside the bedroll and left the door open. Erik finished sweeping dirt and debris into the pan with struggle and dumped it outside. The man was walking toward the house carrying a bird that Erik couldn't readily identify.

"What are you doing?" The man asked tersely as he entered the cabin.

"I'm just cleaning up a bit. I swept and now I was going to stack some wood inside," Erik replied uneasy.

The man didn't acknowledge the response. He laid the bird on the counter and said, "come wash your arm. Do it better than yesterday."

Erik retrieved a bowl from the cabinet and prepared his own wash water. He scrubbed more vigorously to clean the remaining crust of blood off his skin as well as the iodine stains. He still winced but the pain was more manageable. This time Erik poured his own iodine over the arm after the man uncapped the bottle. He helped tie a new bandage.

"Do you really think I need to see a doctor about this? It feels a lot better than it did, even after just one day," Erik asked the man.

He sat at the table and thought. "Yes. You should have that treated by a professional."

Erik looked concerned. He asked the man, "would you see a doctor if it was your arm?"

The man contemplated his answer, again. "No. I probably wouldn't see a doctor for that if it were mine."

"Why should it be different for me?"

The man looked at Erik. "Maybe your life is more worth saving."

Erik was speechless.

"Who sent you here?" The man asked.

Erik looked at the floor and back up. "I worked for a man named Bill Wheeler in Anchorage. I worked at his shop there. I was having a lot of trouble at home and needed to get an escape plan ready. One of his friends, Herb, I never learned his last name, he told me about Andy, or you, or whoever, and said if I was in a bad enough spot that I needed to run, that he was the guy to find. But, at this point, I don't even know if Andy is a real person or who you are or if this is some giant goddamned practical joke."

The man took a breath and looked at Erik. "You must have been real special to Herb and Bill for them to tell you about me and this place." He took another deep breath. "We'll keep an eye on your arm. If it doesn't get a lot better real soon, we are going to take you in. Their word goes a long way with me so they must have wanted you to come here for some good reason. You can stay over there where you slept. It doesn't look like you take much room."

"Is your name Andy?" Erik asked.

"That is what they call me."

11

A new peace permeated the wilderness as the gouge upon the young man's flesh healed. Though a scar remained in its place, function returned with new vigor.

Scars all across the land were blanketed with snow and ice. The perpetually changing season revolved once again. The sun, once persistent across the sky, fell behind the rugged mountains for the last time. This land will not feel its warmth again for many weeks.

~

Erik cleaned the table and began to wash dishes after finishing breakfast. Andy donned a heavy parka and hat. Both appeared to be made by hand. Erik said, "Andy, I want to go with you today."

He looked at the young man. "Okay. Then get your muks on. You can use the snowshoes hanging over there," he said pointing to the far wall.

Erik quickly hung the washrag he was using and left everything in the sink. He put on the gifted boots and jacket and followed Andy outside.

Together they left the warmth of the cabin for a trek across the harsh territory. They did not seem to follow any set trail as Erik was coming to understand. Andy stopped frequently to check traps he had previously set. There did not seem to be any pattern between where he placed the traps but each was unique and deliberate in placement.

The freshly broken trail led Erik out of the dense forest into thickets of brush. Then, by the guiding light of the northern aurora, he exited the wilderness and walked up a steady ridgeline leading to an outlook exposing the entire mountain range. Silhouettes of vast peaks from the Alaska range crossed a great valley and continued with those of the Wrangells. Glaciers reflected green hues from the dancing night sky. Erik's eyes followed the line of rocky spirits to Mt. Saint Elias in the farthest reach of the horizon. He asked no questions of his guide and Andy offered no answers. Nothing need be said.

~

The two men returned to the cabin after several hours of checking the empty line. Erik dished a hearty soup for supper and placed the bowls on the table to cool.

"Andy, I have a question," Erik said. "I see the picture on your desk when I sweep the floors. Who is the picture of?"

Andy stopped eating his soup and put his bowl back on the table. He sat for a moment but didn't look confused by the question. He looked up to Erik with a peculiar expression, maybe one of complex sadness. He stood up from the table, walked to his room, and closed the door behind him.

Erik felt uncertain of what happened. He collected the two bowls of half-eaten soup and cleaned the table. His appetite was gone.

~

The old man sat at his typewriter, transcribing his deepest thoughts. He opened the door to the darkest room in his basement and entered the space that held his darkest agony. He walked through a field of grass and flowers and all heavenly things flowing over rolling hills. Not far ahead he heard the laughter of a child and saw the smile of a beautiful woman. She called to him with her smile and he came running. He ran through the field and toward her. She picked up the child playing at her feet and held him in her arms. They both looked at the man and wore expressions of excitement. *Daddy is home!* the child told his mother. The man ran and kept running but the beautiful woman and her child never got closer. The man looked again through the field but nothing was changing. He ran harder and faster and breathed heavier and shallower. The pollen of the flowers began to burn on his skin as his legs moved through them. The summer breeze held a stench of rotting flesh in his nose and he could not rid it. He ran faster and he ran harder toward them but they were yet farther away. The skies became grey and black above him roiling with acrid smoke. His hands rashed and blistered as he swung them more intensely with each sprinting step. With the last of his strength he dove for the woman and her child. He floated closer to them with arms stretched forward and hands open. The woman held her son close with one hand and opened the other hand to the man. Just as he grabbed her hand, it faded to dust in the man's fingers. Her hand disintegrated and her arm crumpled and turned to dust as the man fell on the ground near her feet. The earth around him was ablaze and the woman and her child were replaced with ash structures. The man cried but no sound was made. Screams carried in the wind and death singed his nostrils. He laid on his back and called for the woman again. With the last of his strength, he held his shaking hand to the sky and saw it catch fire before everything went black.

Andy woke from his dream out of breath and in a panic. He saw the page in front of him lighted by the orange glow of his lantern. He pulled the page out from the typewriter and folded it several times. He placed it on the desk between the typewriter and a scrapbook open to pictures of a young family enjoying a picnic. He flipped the page over to the next but could look no more. He wiped his nose and eyes with his sleeve, laid on his bed, closed his eyes and saw his family once again.

~

Erik slept hard. Harder than usual. The fire was dead and the cabin was cold. He forced himself out from his blankets and started a new fire from a few embers under the ash.

He sat at the table in his coat and tried to make sense of the night before. He saw Andy's door was open and looked to see if he was still asleep. Nothing. He pushed the door a little farther and confirmed the bed was empty. He started to close the door but stopped. Erik stepped into the room to again look at the picture he knew. It was still on the desk in its usual place but now a photo album laid beside it. The page was turned to a newspaper clipping. He read the article and instantly felt sick.

PLANE CRASH IN BROOKS
TWO DEAD ONE MISSING

A picture of wreckage was below it. Twisted frame and sheared aluminum was almost unrecognizable as the plane it once formed. He read the story.

Fairbanks residents Andrew and Victoria Wright were involved in a plane crash Thursday morning. Victoria, a traveling nurse for several northern villages and her pilot husband were flying on her routine route. Victoria (34) and their son also in the plane, Samuel (8), were both killed. Andrew (37) is still missing. Officials have not yet issued an official cause but speculate weather may have been a factor. Andrew was a seasoned pilot with more than a decade of experience in the bush, friends of the family tell the paper.

Erik looked at the several pictures that followed. There were two of the wreckage taken from the scene and another one that showed a man in a hospital bed heavily bandaged.

He flipped the book back to the page he found it on and closed the bedroom door to where it was. Erik sat in front of the stove and held back grief for a family he never knew.

~

By evening Andy returned. He opened the door and a flurry of snow came in behind him. He removed his jacket and came up to Erik. "Erik, since you are all healed up, I think it might be time for you to move on. There are plenty of construction crews in Delta and Fairbanks that could use good help. I could get you some names and they'd probably pay cash to keep you off the books." He didn't look at Erik but could feel his eyes on him.

"What?" Erik squeaked. "I don't want to leave here. I don't want to go back there!"

"We all have to do things we don't want to do, kid. You have been a help around here but it is time for you to move on to your own life."

"I want a life here, out here!"

"I understand that but I don't have a way to keep you here. You need to be in school and making something of yourself. You're a smart kid, you'll find something to do that's better than being a hermit in the woods on government land."

"I have no where else to go. This is the only place I have lived and actually lived! I'm not going back to that trash they pass for civilization. They are selling me a Bill of Goods that is nothing but lies and debauchery and I don't want it!" Erik said.

"Listen, kid. You are sounding pretty ungrateful. I took you in when I could have left you to die. I fed you and clothed you when I could have let you starve and freeze. I don't need you but I let you stay. Now, it is time for you to find some other place to stay and wherever that is isn't my problem."

Erik stood. His face was red and eyes were wet. He slid on his gifted muks and went outside and sat in the middle of the clearing down from the cabin. He sat and watched the aurora-lighted sky for a time.

After what felt like hours, Andy came up behind Erik and sat in the snow next to him. He handed him a metal cup with steam pouring from it. "Tea?"

Erik took the cup and held it in his hands. His fingers were numb and the cup felt like it scalded his skin as his nerves came back to life.

"What do you see?" Andy asked. He took a sip from his own cup.

"I'm just... feeling small," Erik answered.

"Tell me more."

"I look up at the sky and I see so much. Such a wide space and the aurora weaving its way through the constellations. I feel like, how can I have any importance next to those things? Like I am so small and inferior, like I am worthless in this world."

"Erik, you have far more worth in this world than can be described with words. It may not feel like you are very important and maybe you are not doing anything important, but it doesn't mean you can't start doing important things. People who are afraid of dying haven't had anything to live for. Just because a man has worth doesn't mean he has expressed that worth. It is like having a lottery ticket for a million dollars. Until he cashes it in he doesn't have any money to his name. If a man has the potential to do good and important things, he will have worth in this world once he does those things but not a moment before."

"Am I capable of doing anything important?" Erik asked.

"I have known few people who were more capable. You have done some good but you have a lot more to go. You are young. You have an entire lifetime ahead of you but that shouldn't give you the sense that you can lollygag and float through life like so many other men."

Erik thought for a moment. "I really would like to stay here for a while more. Maybe stay through winter and I can move on in spring, if you'll have me stay?"

"I could probably use some help on the line. I'm not sure how many winters I have left, anyway," Andy's voice faded with the tail of a shooting star.

Erik looked at him. "What do you mean?"

"I'm getting old, Erik. My health isn't what it used to be. All candles burn out after long enough and I burned my wick hotter than a lot of others. I'm just getting old." He watched the aurora for a while longer. He thought he heard a child laughing and smiled.

"You know, you remind me a lot of my son. Sam would have been about your age now, too."

Erik looked at Andy. "I am sorry about your family."

"I'm sorry, too. I really miss them." He continued his fond memory. "Come inside. There's something I want to give you."

They both stood up and wiped the snow off their trousers and walked back to the cabin.

Andy came out from his room and handed Erik a knife. "This was my father's belt knife. An old man made it for him when he was a boy working on the river boats. The handle is walrus ivory. I always hoped I could give it to my son but... that isn't going to happen. I don't know anyone else who might understand it. I want you to keep it and use it when you check the line."

Erik wiped away a new round of tears. "Andy, I..." He lost his words.

"You're welcome. It is more important what you do with that knife than the knife itself. By itself it's just some metal and bone. It's what you do with it that makes it special."

"I'll use it like it was meant to be used," Erik said.

"Good. Now get some sleep. I want you to check the line by yourself tomorrow. I trust you can find all the traps by now."

~

What a beautiful thing... Erik thought as he walked through the frozen scene. Birch and willow were coated in white crystalline structures. Blue-grey ice crept between the banks of a small, shallow creek. His breath was visible with each exhalation and with each inhalation the air stung his throat and lungs. Moisture from the air warmed by Erik's core settled around his hood and built a ring of ice around his face.

Each step in the knee-deep snow was deliberate. Each branch bent out of the way was deliberate. Each breath was deliberate.

Erik followed a rough trail but it offered little assistance to the young man as he checked each trap on the line. While some men employ dogs or machines to travel between stops, no such aide existed for the man who runs this path. Erik continued through the woods and watched the frozen scene around him for clues. The man who runs this path changes his route often. While he begins and ends in the same place he finds new wonder, new scenes, new friends, new foes.

The first of many traps was empty. Erik dusted the snow and reset the spring, then left the trap more inviting than how he found it. This process was repeated several times.

In the second half of the two mile route, Erik continued at a slower pace. *What a beautiful thing this is. All of it. Beautiful. But is it meant for me? I am here enjoying this heavenly place but what have I done to earn this?*

What have I done to deserve this? Why not someone else? Why not anyone else? Is it right for me to be enjoying such beauty frozen in time when so many others are burning?

Erik approached the next trap lost in thought. He neared a familiar tree when something unfamiliar jumped beside it. The sudden motion surprised him and Erik fell backwards into the soft white mattress of snow. He stumbled back and to his knees swinging his rifle forward. Now packed with snow, he brought the gun to his shoulder but had to work to get his mitten into the lever-grip. He focused on the object in front of him. A black wall of fur. Only two white eyes distinguished its outline from the dusky background it was silhouetted against.

He looked at the wolf and saw its front right paw caught. He relaxed slightly at the mild safety and resumed his breath. The animal had obviously gnawed at its foot, a red tint stained the snow around the site. Erik continued to look at the wolf and he watched it for some time over the iron sights of his rifle. Behind learned eyes, he recognized a creature of the forest. *I knew this day would come,* Erik thought. He lined the sights on his target, held his breath, and squeezed pressure with his gloved finger until his shoulder felt the recoil. The beast bowed and fell without a sound.

~

Andy laid in his bed long into the morning. The layers of damp blankets he rested on were uncomfortable against his clammy skin but it was the best relief he could find. Andy wiped his forehead again and worked to his side before standing up. He took heavy steps to the outhouse quickened by sudden urgency. Andy sat on the wooden seat and felt his insides twist and turn. He clenched his arms against his core and bent over with each agonizing attack. The old man stood and replaced his trousers once he felt momentary relief. He turned to see the outcome of the internal war. "Oh, God. What a foul mess," he called the brown and red slurry.

Andy walked back to the cabin slowly on this return. With difficulty he wafted air beneath his overcoat to remove the pungent odor that clung to his clothes. Inside, he stoked the fire and sat near the stove.

~

"Andy!" Erik called with excitement. "Come see this, Andy!"

Andy came out from the cabin as Erik dragged his prize near the door. "Wow. That is quite the catch."

"Yeah. It was hell trying to get it back but I did it," Erik replied.

"That you did. Now take her over to the skinning rack and we'll get you set up. Have you skinned a wolf before?"

"No, never."

"Okay. Well, it is already starting to freeze and I don't want to hang this girl inside the house. So, get it strung up and I'll talk you through it."

Erik tugged at the rope to get the wolf off the ground. Its weight was nearly matched with his. Once he was set, Andy guided him through each cut.

"Alright now, easy around the paw. It is a skill, not a race," Andy described.

When the job was completed, it was late into the evening. The area was lit by lantern but the glow did not reach far.

"That was a pretty fine job you did for your first time. How's about we take a trip into town tomorrow and see what your prize is worth?" Andy asked.

"Do you think that is safe? What if someone recognizes me and turns me in?" Erik worried.

"We aren't going anywhere you've been before. No one is going to know you from Adam. These are good people we're seeing. Don't you worry a bit," he replied.

~

Erik rolled the wolf skin tight and tied the bundle onto his packboard. The two men left early before the late-winter sun rose in the sky. Andy led their slog by memory.

"Are you doing okay? You're slowing down a lot," Erik said at a half-pace behind Andy.

"I'm just tired is all. Don't worry about it." He picked up his speed for a short time before feeling out of breath. The two men continued at a rhythmic pace.

The sun was now above the horizon behind the great Alaska range. With the increasing visibility, Erik recognized their approximate location by the ridge to his south and could make out a few dilapidated structures ahead of them. Without speaking, Andy kicked built up snow and ice away from the door of one shed and opened it. "Come here and give me a hand," he called from inside.

Erik's eyes adjusted inside the small shed and helped Andy push a snowmachine through the open doorway. It appeared very old by the amount of scratches and fading of the plastic fender and cracks on the foam seat.

"Here we go," Andy said to himself from inside the shed.

He stepped out and filled its plastic gas tank from the metal fuel can he had stashed. With the shed closed and sled ready, Andy gave three hard pulls on the rope but the motor did not start. Andy held himself up by the handlebar and coughed as he breathed the cold air quickly.

"Here, Andy, let me," Erik said. He grabbed the starter rope handle before Andy could respond. He pulled a dozen times before the tired motor coughed to life. He caught a quick glimpse of Andy's pale face as they mounted the sled.

In ten minutes they covered the same distance by snowmachine what took more than an hour by foot. Andy drove the sled cautiously down the middle of the icy tunnel of willows bending with snow weight marking the designated public trail.

After what felt like hours of wind on Erik's face, with ice on his eyelashes and snot running from his nose, Andy slowed as they approached an intersection. The trail crossed the paved highway in a four-way, each option leading north and south, east and west. He eased the sled onto the maintained path which ran parallel to the highway. He again picked up speed and pushed a new frigid stream against their faces.

At high-noon the sun shed little light on the northern frontier. Street lights never turned off. They lighted the downtown strip of the oncoming town struggling to survive on the frozen tundra.

Andy parked the sled in front of a short row of shops. All four storefronts appeared open with activity inside and each had a Western-style facade and touristy name. They both dismounted and Andy led them inside.

The Interior Trading Post

A wall of warm air met Erik and melted the ice clinging to his eye lashes and along his upper lip. A familiar aroma of sweet tobacco and leather brushed his cheeks and warmed his face.

"How ya doin' Andy?" A jolly Native man called. He stood up from his chair next to wood stove placed in the middle of the room. An old woman next to him smiled and nodded but stayed in her seat and held a tin cup of coffee.

"Hey, Larry. Time's takin' its toll," he replied weakly. "How are you feeling, Mary? Legs still giving you fits?"

"Mary is having more bad days than good, I'm afraid," Larry answered for her. She smiled again and looked back to the stove.

"I'm sorry to hear that," Andy said.

"Well who is the new guy? What's your name, young man?" Larry sounded like a Santa Claus voice-over and warmed the room.

Erik pulled back the hood of his parka and removed his gloves. "My name is Erik," he said awkwardly with numb lips, then held out his hand.

"Why it's good to meet you, Erik. Will you two gentleman come sit and have some coffee?" His grip was uncomfortably strong on Erik's cold hand.

"I'll take you up on the coffee but we aren't going to stay too long," Andy replied.

"Nonsense. Come take a seat and we'll look at your bounty when you're warmed up," the jovial man said.

Both of the guests sipped their coffee and warmed their hands as Larry provided updates on local and world news. Andy accounted for changes in the mountains and updates on trail conditions. After three top-offs, Erik sat his cup on the coffee table and held the arms of the chair with both hands to still himself from the caffeine-induced shakes and vertigo.

"Well, Larry. I brought Erik here up to see what you would give him for his wolf."

Larry looked at the skin rolled and tied to the packboard leaning against the counter. "Let's take a look and see how you done, kid."

Erik untied the roll and laid the skin on the counter. It was still a little frozen in the middle of the roll. Larry looked it over, inspecting the skin and the fur. "Tell me, Erik. How long have you been skinning?"

"Not long at all, I've just practiced on a few small things. This is my first wolf. Well, my first animal of any real size," he replied.

Larry looked up and glanced between Erik and Andy. "Are you sure you didn't do this and now you're trying to pull the wool over my eyes?" He asked to Andy. "This is an outstanding specimen," Larry emphasized.

"Nope, it was all me, Larry. Andy helped guide me but the knife never left my hand," Erik said proudly.

"My, oh my. You keep this up and you'll be an outstanding woodsman. I have guys that've come in here for a decade and still can't get their darn lines right. This, this here is just outstanding considering your experience. There is a little bit of chop here," he pointed, "but it won't make a big difference. I'd say we have a top-notch grade here."

Erik and Larry negotiated their price and shook hands over it. The balance was settled, then Erik and Andy bundled up for their journey home.

12

So far from home am I, yet where I long for is nearby;
    I left that place so long ago, I cannot remember why.
No! I shall not bear false witness.
        I shall not tell a lie!
    I know why I ran so fast,
        if I hadn't I'd likely die.
Die a death complete with valor?
    Not even a thought, a prayer, a sound on the wind.
O God, why must I live and suffer so?
        Why must I stay here, can I not go?
    I see living ghosts with opaque eyes,
        I see hollow beasts with rotting cores.
    When will I see streets of gold, rivers of honey?
I do not belong in this realm of the wicked,
    so why have You placed me here?
O God, why have You picked me?
        Is it for punishment? Is this a game?
    I don't know where I'm going
        but I see whence I came.
I look behind me and cower.
        How am I here?
    I see two lions on the road, Hungry and Mean.
        But I passed by them unscathed and still clean!
    One stood on his legs but could not take a step,
        the other just sat there, nor even looked up.
    Were You beside me placing my foot?
        Or were You behind me, Your breath I mistook?
When I arrive to wherever I'm going,
    I can be sure of where I have been.
If I had not suffered nor hurt,
    lived with no comfort sleeping on dirt,
        then how would I know what is this great pleasure,
    to stand on tall mountains, Your hand on my shoulder.

"Are you coming today?" Erik asked as he laced his muks.

Andy sat at the table and watched the young man don his winter protection. "Oh, I guess so."

"If you stay home much more I am afraid it is you who will be getting lost," Erik joked.

"Oh now, I know what you're doing. Don't get your britches in a wad, I'll go with you."

Erik led the team of two in their typical non-direct style. Before walking up the hill to the crest of the ridge, he first led Andy down the creek to inspect the beaver dam.

"What a beautiful creation they have," Andy remarked. Erik smiled and listened to unseen activity from within the beaver house.

"Yeah. Even here in the coldest and darkest time of the year, they still have a warm place to call home. It is like, no matter how dangerous is it outside there is a safe place to return to."

"It is the creature who wanders alone that walks with risk," Andy said.

Erik turned up the hill and started the climb from the low beaver pond up and beyond the tree line. He slowed his pace as the distance between him and Andy increased. He turned and walked back a short distance.

"What's wrong?" Erik asked.

Andy grunted. "Nothing. I am just," he breathed hard, "just feelin' a little weak today."

"You are moving really slow."

"Yeah, old men do that when their feelin' weak," Andy said sarcastically.

Erik lead a direct route and both finished the loop, Andy with great effort.

~

"I heard you running to the outhouse last night. You were up most of the night," Erik said at breakfast.

"Yeah. I was there," Andy replied.

"You're sick. You are pale. You haven't had color in your face for a month," Erik said sadly. "Are you dying?"

Andy played with his food but never raised his spoon. He paused. "I am getting old. I don't have as much energy as I used to. I've also had a real bad bug for a while. Last night it just gave me fits. Don't think much more about it."

"I want you to go in and see the doctor."

"I don't need a doctor. Just give me time and I'll be good as can be." Andy didn't make eye contact.

Erik didn't speak again that morning. He cleaned up from breakfast, fed the stove, and suited up for his daily check of the trap line. He did not wait for his haggard companion.

~

The cabin was empty when Erik returned. He stoked the wood stove and warmed his hands before skinning two marten and a lynx caught that day. He started to prepare supper. A note laid next to the sink:

Went to town. Back tomorrow. Maybe two.

~

"Back so soon?" Larry asked from behind the counter. He put down the needle he was working through a tanned hide and gave his visitor full attention.

"Yeah. I have some business I need to take care of. I need to ask you a favor," Andy said. He had closed the door behind him but didn't step farther in.

"Anything you need," Larry returned. He leaned on the counter paying close, curious attention to his friend.

"I am going to be leaving for a while and Erik is going to take over for some time. He will need help ordering supplies and caching food. He doesn't know the logistics of it, yet. I need to know you will help him with those things until he figures it out." Andy was speaking slow, each word calculated and predetermined.

"Of course, Andy," Larry replied. He understood the words but the meaning was a mystery.

"I also need you to stay quiet about him," he glanced at Larry's wife. She sat by the stove and watched the flames. "He is a runaway and probably on the Trooper's radar. When you deal with him continue running it under my name."

"I'll do that, Andy, but where are you going?"

He paused. "I'm going to see some relatives. It is a long trip."

Larry nodded and watched the door after his lifelong friend left.

C

Lay not up for yourselves treasures upon earth,
where moth and rust doth corrupt,
and where thieves break through and steal:

But lay up for yourselves treasures in heaven,
where neither moth nor rust doth corrupt,
and where thieves do not break through nor steal:

For where your treasure is, there will your heart be also.
Matthew 6:19-21 KJV

Behold the fowls of the air:
for they sow not, neither do they reap, nor gather into barns;
yet your heavenly Father feedeth them.
Are ye not much better than they?

There is that maketh himself rich,
yet hath nothing:
there is that maketh himself poor,
yet hath great riches.
Proverbs 13:7 KJV

13

"Only a few more days left for the season," Erik said at breakfast. "I really am glad to be here."

"I am glad you are here, too. Seems like each night gets a little lonelier. Each winter gets a little colder. You have brought a lot of great company to this tired old man."

"You aren't that old, why do you keep saying that?" Erik asked.

"Because whether you like it or not, it is true. You'll understand it. Bones creak. Joints ache. Muscles doesn't move as fast. Mind gets slow." He chuckled and stirred his soup. "When I was a kid, there was this old hag that lived down the street and boy was she mean. Every day she sat out in her rocker and just watched. She was always scanning around looking for someone to yell at so one day my buddies and me decided to give her somethin' to do." Erik leaned in and grinned. "We were playin' catch in the street and having a gay time when my old pal Dennis got the bright idea to hit the ball right in her direction. That ball made a b-line right through her kitchen window and she just about fell backwards. Boy, she just started hollarin'. Of course, Dennis was probably in the next county over by the time I figured out what had just occurred in front of me. All the other kids must've known something was up because when I looked around everyone else had gone an' run off, too." Erik was laughing out loud and put down his spoon. "So here I was standing in the middle of the street with this raging bull about to lay hell down upon me as she came flying across her yard. Actually, she was so crippled up she couldn't shuffle but one bitty step at a time and I could have just walked away but I was a man of honor back then so I stood there and waited for her. It is also possible I might have just been too scared right out of my shorts to even think about moving but I'll go with the honor part. So here she was waving her cane in my face and mouthing all kinds of profanities. Fortunately or unfortunately she did not have her teeth in so I could not understand but a word she said but I pretty well got the point. Finally she slowed down enough that I understood what she was asking and that was 'why did we hit a ball right through her window?' I don't know why I said what I said but I squeaked out 'why, Mrs. Paget, we just made your house look as old as you are.' I can't hardly think of a worse thing a boy could have said in that moment but she squinted up real tight and leaned in and said 'wrinkles is things of beauty'. Well, I don't know if that is true or not but I do know that you never want to be the slowest runner in a group."

Erik went from wiping tears of laughter to a dumbfounded look that almost hurt his face. He looked across the table at Andy sitting content in his memory and said, "what the hell does that have to do with anything we were talking about?"

Andy came back to attention and met Erik's gaze. "Oh," he said and scratched his beard. "I don't know."

Erik was speechless. He looked at him a moment then stood up and carried the dishes into the kitchen. He finished his chores and suited up to check the line.

~

That night was quiet. Andy stayed in his room and typed by candle. Erik left him alone and read by the stove. This pattern continued through the week.

"Erik, I have a favor to ask you," Andy said at supper. "After you take care of the line tomorrow and stash all of the traps will you take everything in to Larry's? It will be kind of tight with both of us and the skins and I think I'd just as soon stay home."

"Yeah, I can do that. Larry will probably miss not seeing you. You sure you don't want to go?"

"I am sure. I saw him not long ago. Life around here doesn't change that fast, you know," Andy said. "I trust you to get a fair deal for everyone. Anyway, Larry knows he couldn't pull a fast one on you even if he tried."

"All thanks to you," Erik complimented.

"I also have a few letters I would like you to send out. I'll get them all stamped tonight and in a bundle you can just leave at the Post Office."

"Sure. I can do that. Do you need anything? You are still so pale. Maybe I can get something from the drug store?" Erik asked.

"Maybe just a fresh tin of coffee will do."

Erik didn't push the matter.

~

"Be safe. You have done this enough times you know where you are going," Andy said as Erik donned his parka.

"I'm more concerned about you getting into trouble than me," Erik replied. He flashed a smile but returned to a neutral face. Something was different but he couldn't figure out what.

"You have the hides on your packboard, you have the letters. Okay. I'll have everything sorted out by the time you get back."

"What do you mean?" Erik asked.

"I mean that there are some things I want to change around here and I aim to have everything the way it ought to be in short order. You'll see."

Without thinking Erik gave the man a hug. He looked at the man's peaceful face once more then stepped out and closed the door behind him. Erik hoisted his packboard onto his back and embarked on his journey.

~

Snow was starting to melt in town and stretches of trail were showing dark mud patches. Erik eased the snowmachine along the gravel road and parked it in a familiar spot.

"How'ya doin' there, Erik?" Larry asked in his typical jovial manner.

"I am great, today. How are you doing?" Erik warmly replied.

"Well I couldn't be better now that you're here. What do you have for me?"

"I've got the year-end marten, lynx... a couple hare, and... oh, a beaver."

"A beaver? I didn't thinking you guys were running a line in the pond," Larry asked confused.

"We aren't. I don't know what this fella was doing but he made his way over to the conibear and stuck his head in so far he got stuck. Andy said he has never seen anything like it. We still can't figure it out but he's in the bag, anyway."

"Huh. That does sound like the darndest thing but hey, legal is legal." Larry looked at the horns mounted around the room. "Or at least just keep saying it is."

They both inspected the skins and negotiated the grading and price until each man was satisfied.

"Anything else I can do for you, Erik?"

"Nope. Just need to pick up some coffee and drop this bundle of letters off."

"If you want I can drop them off for you. I'll be headed over in a bit anyway," Larry said.

"Oh, sure. That will save me a stop." Erik pulled the bundle out and laid it on the counter.

Larry picked up the bundle and thumbed through them checking stamps. "Oops, this one here doesn't have any postage." He pulled the rubber band off and set the letter aside. Larry grabbed the book of stamps from beside the till and put one on the letter. "There we go," he said. "That's queer. This letter is addressed to you."

"What?" Erik said as he looked at the letter. "You're right. That's weird. Think I should open it?"

"It's addressed to you. No sense in mailing something to yourself unless you're some kind of lonely."

"Alright. Sorry you wasted a stamp, Larry."

Larry shrugged his shoulders and smiled.

Erik opened the letter, looked at Larry, then read it aloud:

Dear Erik,

You have probably figured out by now that I am not well. I keep thinking it can't get much worse… and then it does. It can be denied no longer. Some demon has worked its way inside me and is doing a real number. Cancer or some damn thing. Getting close to the end of my time here and decided to get things in order.

I am sorry to do this by letter but it will be for the best. I hope you will not waste time being angry or depressed. Beyond an appropriately short period of grieving, it is pointless and will be agony in the long run if we do not understand and accept the fact that nothing is ever perfect and few things happen the way we wish. The world is not a fair, safe place. Sadly, so many folks who spend their lives fighting this so often lose sight of the joy, peace, and wonder to be found in a simple life, accepting reality the best they can.

The fact is I am dying. No amount of sorrow or resentment will change that. Before I leave this world behind, I must settle some business. First, the cabin and what remains of my estate is yours. You are all that remains of my fallen family tree. Eugene has my papers and will hold everything in trust until you are of age. Larry will get you his information. There isn't much but it will help you get a fresh start. You have been walking uphill for too long. You have earned a break. Second, there are some things I want to share with you.

I was 7 years old when my grandfather was dying in the hospital. On his last day, my grandmother saw how upset I was when I had to say my "goodbyes". She pulled me in close and said "don't say 'goodbye' give your grandpa a 'see you later'". I still believe in "see you laters" because our souls never die. Our conversations never end. I can still close my eyes and have those conversations with Victoria and Samuel and all of my friends and family that died long ago. I can hear their thoughts, ask their wisdom and guidance, and have a great visit with them. Sometimes the sound of their voice gets fuzzy as the years pass but their words and their spirit pervade.

Each terrible day you struggle to find the strength to put one foot in front of the other, I will be there to help pick you up, dust off your shoulders, and give you a swift kick in the butt.

Two boys were walking down the sidewalk. Bothers, one the age of 12, the other 10. Both walked with their heads down and phones out. Behind them sat Elias, proud against the sky, blue and purple and covered in snow. The rock glowed in the late sun. The boys did not chase each other. Neither one teased nor poked nor pestered. Each chose virtual stimulation over bruises and scrapes. Neither experienced God's world. How many new ideas are lost because the conversation never happened?

To put my life lessons in a nutshell, personal responsibility is, of course, the foundation. But that's a tough row to hoe for most of us so I won't bother with a Part Two. Until then, live this moment in life. It is one pin-point of time on the horizon of eternity that will never happen again. I only recently connected my thoughts of political freedom, personal freedom, and freedom in nature. To be reliant on nobody but myself... to so closely be connected with the food on my table, the water in my glass, wood in my stove, and the roof over my head. "Those who do not work, do not eat." I chose this route many years ago and still hold it true. What changed from then to now is I accept I can no longer do it alone. God created us social beings. Become sick or injured, even to a mild degree, and see how independent you really feel. Spend your fruitful years building good, based relationships so that when hard times come you will have a shoulder to cry on. The trick is to build these as partners equally yoked, nobody in control of the other. You will have no stronger relationship than with God. I recommend you making friends with Him.

On failure:

If failure is to "not meet a previously stated goal", then might that not depend on how realistic the goal was? By this definition, not winning the lottery would be a failure. But only minimal research on the issue will reveal that winning the lottery is fool's play, so why choose that as a goal? It is doomed to fail. One man's failure is another man's spur to effort and it is likely not seen as a failure at all. Also, I believe it is the will of God to allow some men to be failures in life to serve as examples for others. "Honor thy father and thy mother" Honor, respect, dignify. All these do not mean "worship". It means do not let him die in vain letting his failures go to the grave without recognition, for those who disregard the failures of his father shall never know the difference. Look in the mirror: the normal response to failure is avoidance and rejection when it ought to be acknowledgement and curiosity.

Introspection is valuable and worth doing often. Thoughts for summer hikes and winter trapline checks? Snowy days when you can't get out? Meditation time should be something you plan and look forward to. Think about your goals, your expectations, the resources you have or can acquire. Hopes and dreams are wonderful things but must be balanced with reality. It is a hard call sometimes. We make mistakes. Good judgment is the product of surviving a lot of bad judgment (with follow-up!). A question to ask yourself: Do you trust yourself? Do you even like yourself? Sometimes "trust" and "like" are misplaced, especially of ourselves, but self-trust and self-like are a necessary part of a meaningful life. If you don't trust and like yourself to at least a moderate degree, that might be where you need to start.

Plan A rarely goes as planned. The same goes for Plan B through Z. Plans are a starting point and are useful (if not a prerequisite) but rarely remain the same after the first step.

Upon your return, you will find the cabin empty. There are two routes in front of me. The first route is one of lights and sirens and a mad dash to what I can only describe as living hell. The second route is one final walk alone with God in the only place I feel at peace.
    When I saw my child for the first time, I knew that I was blessed.
    When I saw you for the last time, I knew that I was ready.
    When I see my family again, I will know that I am home.
Love should be nurtured, celebrated, enjoyed wherever it is found. Genuine love is the best thing life has to offer. Don't let anyone tell you otherwise. You have my love, no strings attached.

Winter has been so long, it is time for this bird to fly away.
Live, so you can afford to die.

Maybe someday we shall meet again.

See you later.

Andy

And the light shineth in darkness;
and the darkness comprehended it not.
John 1:5 KJV

EPILOGUE

A man smoked for 30 years and was then diagnosed with terminal lung cancer. Which cigarette was the single one that gave the man cancer? Was it the 10,000[th] cigarette? Was it the 20,000[th] cigarette? Was it the 5th? One of the cigarettes was the single one that tipped the scales and caused the man lung cancer but he doesn't know which single cigarette to blame.

God gives man one struggle he cannot fight alone, one burden he cannot bear without His support. That is man's opportunity to:
1) pray for God's help; or,
2) fail as his own god.
Many are called but few answer.

Each day you have a new opportunity to begin the rest of your life. Which path will you chose?

> The Lord is my shepherd; I shall not want.
> He maketh me to lie down in green pastures:
> he leadeth me beside the still waters.
> He restoreth my soul:
> he leadeth me in the paths of righteousness
>   for his name's sake.
> Yea, though I walk through the valley of the shadow of death,
> I will fear no evil: for thou art with me;
> thy rod and thy staff they comfort me.
> Thou preparest a table before me
> in the presence of mine enemies:
> thou anointest my head with oil; my cup runneth over.
> Surely goodness and mercy shall follow me
> all the days of my life:
> and I will dwell in the house of the Lord for ever.
>   Psalm 23 KJV

To my Brothers,   C
you know who you are:

I thank my God upon every remembrance of you,
always in every prayer of mine making request for you all with joy,
for your fellowship in the gospel from the first day until now,
being confident of this very thing,
that He who has begun a good work in you will complete it
until the day of Jesus Christ;
just as it is right for me to think this of you all,
    because I have you in my heart,
    inasmuch as both in my chains
    and in the defense and confirmation of the gospel,
you all are partakers with me of grace.
For God is my witness,
how greatly I long for you all
with the affection of Jesus Christ.

Philippians 1:3-8 NKJV

THE WRITER

Jeremy lives in the mountains where he is never again alone.
Wilt thou be made whole?

The grace of our Lord Jesus Christ be with you all.
Amen.